"The pilot's picking me up on his way back."

Daunted by the grim look on Drew's face, Briar had felt compelled to explain the situation hastily.

"Which will be a week from now, if not longer," he said.

Briar's voice was strangled as she said, "I can't possibly stay here for a whole week."

"You haven't got an option," he said curtly.

Gone was the kindly man she'd known in Singapore. Here in this primeval land was a totally different being.

"You're making the workmen stare at me as if I'm some sort of apparition."

"They're not used to camp followers."

"How dare you!" Briar's hand shot up to slap his face, but with equal speed his fingers caught and circled her wrist with crushing force.

"Try that again," Drew said, gritting his teeth, "and I might forget I'm a gentleman."

Sue Peters grew up in the idyllic countryside of Warwickshire, England, and began writing romance novels quite by chance. "Have a go," her mother suggested when a national writing contest sponsored by Mills and Boon appeared in the local newspaper. Sue's entry placed second, and a career was born. After completing her first romance novel, she missed the characters so much she started another and another.... Now she's as addicted to writing as she is to gardening, which she often does as she's formulating new plots.

Books by Sue Peters

HARLEQUIN ROMANCE
2583—LIGHTNING STRIKES TWICE
2812—NEVER TOUCH A TIGER
2892—ENTRANCE TO EDEN
2915—CAPTURE A NIGHTINGALE
2938—ONE-WOMAN MAN
3018—UNWILLING WOMAN

WEEKEND WIFE
Sue Peters

Harlequin Books

TORONTO • NEW YORK • LONDON
AMSTERDAM • PARIS • SYDNEY • HAMBURG
STOCKHOLM • ATHENS • TOKYO • MILAN
MADRID • WARSAW • BUDAPEST • AUCKLAND

Original hardcover edition published in 1991
by Mills & Boon Limited

ISBN 0-373-03226-9

Harlequin Romance first edition October 1992

WEEKEND WIFE

CHAPTER ONE

IT WAS over.

Briar walked down the three stone steps leading from the courthouse on to the pavement below, carefully taking one step at a time. The metal tips on the heels of her court shoes clicked sharply as they met each step, beating time to her thoughts.

It's over. It's over. It's over.

She should feel glad. She should feel sad. She should feel *something*.

She felt nothing at all. Only empty. It was as if a big block of ice was settled inside her, freezing out her capacity to feel. Later, it would melt, and then the pain would start. But now, at this moment, she was grateful for the numbness. It kept at bay the wild despair that threatened her sanity.

Her solicitor spoke. 'It's all over now. You must put it behind you and make a new life for yourself. That shouldn't prove too difficult.' His smile was warm. 'You're a very attractive woman, Mrs Adamson. Remember that, and don't let this—er—happening destroy your confidence.'

The look in his eyes appreciated her attractiveness, breaking through the impersonal, professional barrier which he had carefully kept erected between them until now.

Briar stiffened. He probably only meant to be kind. She could use some confidence—her own had taken a severe knock. But male appreciation was the last thing she wanted, either now or in the future. Her tone pushed him firmly back behind the barrier.

'Miss Lycett,' she corrected him. 'From now on, I intend to revert to my maiden name.'

'A good idea.' He nodded, accepting the way she felt. 'Your decree nisi will come through in due course. I'll be in touch with you, with the final paperwork and so on, and then you'll feel completely free.'

Free to do what? Briar wondered bitterly.

The question pursued her as she parted company with the solicitor, and walked away from him along the crowded street, her nut-brown curls held determinedly high. She shook hands with her adviser, thanked him mechanically for all he had done to help her, refused his offer of lunch. Mourning her refusal, he stood on the pavement, watching the slight figure walk out of his life.

Poor kid! What was she? Coming up twenty-four, and deserted by a swine of a husband who did not deserve her. Losing her baby on top of it all had been the last straw. He wondered what she would do now.

She was not without courage; he had learned that during their brief acquaintance. He had come to admire the straight hazel gaze, and the plucky tilt to her chin. True, it had faltered when the baby died. She had foundered then, and he had to pull her through the last bit of the court proceedings. But it was over now, and satisfactorily, at least from his point of view.

He wondered how his client viewed it. That clear gaze of hers was intelligent, fearless, and managed to hide a lot of what she was really feeling, deep down inside her.

'Coming for a bit of pub grub, Mac? Got to keep up your strength, you know.' A colleague from the other court slapped him on the shoulder, and the solicitor turned, dragging his eyes away from Briar's retreating back.

'Too right. I've got another case coming up this afternoon.'

It was another divorce case. Feeling suddenly depressed, the lawman turned and walked beside his colleague. Too many divorces. It was the major part of his work these days, sorting out human relationships which had gone sour. It earned him his living, of course. But sometimes, like now, he wished he had opted for another profession.

'Briar Lycett. *Miss* Briar Lycett,' Briar murmured the name over to herself as she walked. The name had once been as familiar to her as her own face in the mirror, and she would now have to get used to using all over again.

Briar Lycett . . . She would never use her married name again. She did not even want to remember what it had been.

She could forgive Philip for what he had done to herself. She could even understand how it was that the handsome, ambitious, and socially very much in demand young stockbroker should find a continually crying baby got on his nerves after a hectic day at the office, and preferred the sophisticated elegance of his girlfriend's flat to his own filled with a tired wife, and a crying baby, even if that baby was his own.

She would never, ever forgive him for what he had said when she had telephoned to let him know that Lucy was in hospital, and desperately ill.

'The doctor says that's why she's always crying, Philip. It's a rare condition, apparently, and once it sets in it's swift-acting. There's nothing they can do for her.'

'In that case, it will save me from having to pay maintenance for her, won't it?'

He had not come to the hospital to see Lucy while there was still time. Nor had he attended the baby's funeral afterwards. He had removed his clothes and personal belongings from the flat, and told Briar brutally,

'OK, so I made a mistake. Family life just isn't me. Let the court settle who's to have what.'

She had not seen him again after that, nor did she want to. But without Philip, and Lucy, she was left with a void of emptiness that had to be filled in somehow. Eventually she would return to her career, but not yet. First of all, she needed time in which to sort herself out, before she was ready to face the world again.

Confidence was a necessary ingredient of her job as a remedial therapist, and Philip's callous behaviour had dealt her own a cruel blow, from which it would take some time to recover.

Of one thing only she could feel certain. She would *never* allow herself to be hurt like that again. She would never trust another man so long as she lived.

She had slapped down a friend's well-meant advice to, 'Forget Philip. You'll meet someone else soon, someone more worthy of you.'

'I'll never marry again. Once was more than enough for me. From now on, I'll go it alone.'

Her friend had thought, What a waste, and cautioned, 'You'll be lonely.'

'I'd rather be single and lonely than married and miserable.'

A street collector walked up now, smiling and shaking a tin hopefully. The notice on the tin said the money was in aid of some disaster or other, Briar could not see what, or where; the rest of the lettering was round the other side of the tin. She felt very much like a disaster area herself at the moment, and the feeling gave her kin, so she stopped and opened her purse.

As her fingers closed around a clutch of coins, the glint of gold from her wedding-ring caught her eye. Impulsively she stripped it off, and added it to the coins, and the collector's smile grew wider as she too caught the glint of gold, and assumed it to be a coin of a good denomination.

Briar wondered what the people who counted the money would think when they found a wedding-ring in their tin. She hoped they would be able to dispose of it for a reasonable sum, to help whatever charity they were collecting for. It was worthless to her.

Nevertheless, her hand felt oddly light without it, when she got home and put the kettle on to make a cup of tea. Food did not appeal to her, but a cup of tea might help to melt some of the ice.

Sipping the comforting brew ten minutes later, she was tempted to ignore the telephone when it rang. It might be one of Philip's friends, curious to know the outcome of the morning's hearing, or one of her own friends, open to offer sympathy. Briar did not want either, but the ringing persisted, threatening to turn her hovering headache into a painful reality if she did not put an end to it. She picked up the receiver.

'Briar Lycett here.' Other people must get accustomed to using her new name as well.

'Hi, Sis! It's Tony.'

The tenseness went out of Briar. Bless Tony! Her brother accepted her name as if she had never used any other. That was the beauty of Tony. He was never curious. He waited until you felt ready to tell him things. And then he did not waste time on useless sympathy. Sensibly, he believed practical support to be the better option, and obliquely he offered it to her now.

'Briar, can you help me out? The Lycett Domestic Rescue Service is in need of being rescued itself! I've got so much work coming in I can't handle it all, with the staff I've got. I need someone I can depend on, quickly. Not to use the machines and do the actual cleaning thing—I need a sort of co-ordinator who'll buzz round between the jobs, doing a bit of PR work, so the customers will feel they're getting attention from the top, so to speak. It works wonders with recommendations.' He paused. 'That is, unless you've already got something lined up for yourself?'

'Not yet. They want me back at the rehabilitation clinic, but I need a bit of space first, to sort myself out. I've just come back from the court.'

'And?'

'It's over, Tony. Now I want to put it behind me and find something—*anything*—that will keep me so busy I shan't have time to think.'

Her desperation sounded clear in her voice, and Tony answered promptly.

'Then come to us. I can promise you won't have a spare minute.'

'How soon do you want me?'

'Now.' He was emphatic. 'As soon as you can sell up and get here.'

'There's nothing to sell. The flat's rented. The local charity shop can have my share of the furniture and fittings.'

Tony whistled. 'They'll think they've won the pools! You've got some good furniture.'

'They're welcome to it.'

Briar did not want any keepsakes. She packed her clothes, rejecting those things, even jewellery, which Philip had given to her. The charity shop could have those too. Carefully she fitted the only photograph she had of her precious baby into the gold locket which was her coming-of-age gift from her parents, and, slipping it safely around her neck under her sweater, she took the flat key back to the agent.

'We'll be glad to have you as a tenant any time, Mrs Adamson,' he assured her, wondering what was causing her hasty departure. She had never been behind with the rent.

'I won't be coming back.'

When Briar reached Warwick, the bustling county town near to which she had been brought up, she felt as if she had never been away. Philip had always despised what he contemptuously described as 'the sticks'. London was the only place which existed for him, but Briar had not realised before how much she missed her home county.

The castle still stood, admiring its time-worn face in the placid waters of the Avon. The slowly shunting traffic in the narrow streets took her past the old half-timbered hospital, dreaming in the sun that had warmed its walls for six hundred years, and the pillarbox, which proudly announced that it belonged to Victoria Regina, greeted her like an old friend, before the traffic-lights changed, and the stream of cars gathered speed and carried her with them towards the outer edge of the town.

In spite of the busy streets, the sense of time-lessness which pervaded the place acted like a balm after the cruel brevity of her marriage and even briefer motherhood. She turned into the yard at the back of her brother's business premises with a feeling of coming home, and the sleek grey Jaguar car which had stood with her in the traffic jam coming through the town swung out and round her, and roared away.

Tony was waiting for her with a pot of freshly brewed tea, and a plate stacked high with some hastily put together cheese sandwiches.

'Help yourself,' he invited, and groaned as the telephone rang.

'It's like this all the time! Everyone wants help right away, if not sooner.' He picked up the receiver. 'Tony Lycett here. Yes, of course, I'll come at once—leave everything. We'll do the coping for you. Go and make yourself a nice cup of tea, and don't worry. I'll be with you in about twenty minutes.'

He put the phone down, and apologised, 'Sorry, Sis, I've got to go. It's an easy one this time—chip pan fire that's spread through the kitchen. The fire brigade have been and put out the flames, but apparently the kitchen's a wreck, and the woman is near to hysterics. Sorry to drop you in at the deep end like this, but if you can hold the fort until I get back...?'

'What about your sandwiches?'

'I've got used to eating in shifts,' Tony grinned. 'Graham should be back soon—he's the foreman. He'll take over, and let you get settled in. But if anyone else rings for help before he gets here be an angel and go out and see what they want, will you? We try to make a point of responding right away to every call, no matter how trivial it is. We get some odd calls at times. But we're slowly building up a reputation for tackling anything that comes our way, no matter how way-out. The funniest one was the herd of goats—but I'll tell you about that another time. The thing is, don't ignore a call, and *never* refuse a job. We're the first in the market in this area, and we want to stay the best. I've got plans for further expansion. One of the big insurance companies is beginning to use our services in connection with their household policies, which is great for the domestic side of our work.'

'Where do you want to expand from there?'

'Into the commercial side, if I can. If I can manage to get a foot in with one of the big firms locally, and get their recommendation, it would be just the breakthrough I need, but it's still got to happen, so keep your eyes open for the big chance.'

'What do I do if a customer calls before your foreman gets back?' Briar looked her alarm.

'Just go out and assess what damage has been done. It could be fire, or flood. Sometimes, in extreme cases, it's sheer wanton vandalism, but fortunately that doesn't happen often. The thing is to reassure the client that we're doing something for them *immediately*. That's why, when you come back, you must bring the curtains with you for cleaning. That way, something is seen to be done straight away. Psychological, of course, but it works wonders for the client's morale, and it's good for our business. It gets us talked about.'

With a wave, he was gone. Mary, the blind telephone operator, laughed through the open door of the ante-room which housed the busy switchboard.

'It's a madhouse, Briar! But you'll get used to it.'

'The place has certainly grown since I went away.'

She gazed out of the office window to the recently extended parking area, now capable of holding at least a dozen vehicles, instead of the three she remembered. A van drew up even as she watched, and the crew jumped out smartly, two men and a woman, all dressed alike in green dungarees.

'That will be Alf and his crew.' The three-horn signal from the van driver warned Mary which crew was back at base.

'We're just in for five minutes, to load up again,' the driver popped his head round the office door, 'then we're off to that job on the outskirts of Leamington Spa. We've got their curtains back from the cleaners, and if we hang them up, and finish off there before we stop for a bite to eat, they'll be back to normal before teatime. The lady of the house will be thankful to have it done. She's got six-month-old twins on her hands.'

The driver nodded in a friendly fashion to Briar, before he too disappeared. She tried not to think of the six-month-old twins, and to push them out of her mind she asked Mary, 'Do they all work at this speed all the time?'

'Mostly,' the telephone operator answered. 'It's amazing how the service has taken on. If you remember, when we first started people regarded us as a gimmick, not to be taken seriously. Now they can see the advantages of having a trained crew descend on them when they've had a fire, or a flood, and get things back to normal in a quarter of the time it would take if they tried to do all the work themselves. So many women go out to work, as well as their husbands; they haven't the time to cope with domestic disasters themselves. We've taken on a decorating team as well, so that we can offer the complete service.

'So I see, from the sign on the side of that van.' Briar read its logo out loud. 'Domestic disasters coped with immediately. No waiting. Leave it all to us. No job too large or too small. Distance no object.' She frowned anxiously. 'I hope Tony can live up to his claims. If he can't he's going to come an awful cropper.'

'Don't worry, he... oh, there goes Alf.' Mary raised a hand to the window which she could not see, as another toot on the horn told her of the crew's departure. 'Here we go again!' She turned back to the switchboard as it began to buzz urgently.

'Lycett Domestic Rescue Service...yes, Miss Lycett is here herself.' Tony had obviously told Mary about her change of name, which was a relief, because it saved her from having to explain. Briar listened interestedly, as Mary continued,

'Yes, she'll come out to you right away. Will she need to bring a plumber with her? No? That's fine. In that case, you can give her all the details when she gets there. Where? I see. She should be with you in about half an hour.'

Mary flicked off the switch and turned to Briar. 'I must say, he sounded pretty cool, not a bit like they usually are. But he says it's very urgent, so it's best not to keep him waiting. The name of the house is the Paddocks. He says it lies well back from the lane, but you'll recognise it by the cartwheel gates at the drive entrance. According to him, your quickest route will be to head out towards Kenilworth, then turn into the lanes about a mile out of town.' Rapidly she repeated the directions she had been given, and Briar nodded.

'I know the house. I used to know the people who lived there, but I expect they've changed since I've been away.'

'He says his name is Steel—Andrew Steel.'

'Then the owners have changed.'

Most things had changed, including herself. But here with Tony she would be kept busy, with no time in which to think, which was what she needed. Gulping down the last of her cup of tea, Briar promised the still untouched stack of sandwiches, 'I'll make short work of you when I get back,' and headed out to her car with Mary's warning ringing in her ears,

'Don't refuse the job, whatever it is. And bring back the curtains with you.'

Briar found the cartwheel gates without difficulty. They had been left propped open, presumably to receive her, and within the prescribed half-hour she braked to a halt on the wide gravel sweep in front of the once-familiar house.

The building appeared to have been extensively altered and enlarged, but she was left with no time in which to take in details. A tall, black-haired figure, somewhere in his early thirties, Briar guessed, and evidently the new owner, peeled himself from off the pillar of a rose arch and strolled across to greet her.

'Andrew Steel,' he confirmed, and held out his hand.

Briar winced at the firmness of his grip. She decided that Mary's description of him as cool was a good one, and wondered why he had called upon them for help. He looked as if he was capable of coping with any disaster himself single-handed, and that with one tied behind his back.

She studied him covertly. She had a feeling that she had seen him somewhere before, but she could not think where. She dismissed the feeling. She had probably bumped into his lookalike somewhere. Andrew Steel was a stranger to her. To know him would be to remember him clearly. His was not a face one was likely to forget.

His surname suited him. The look he bent on her had a steely quality in it, to match the colour of his eyes, and underlined by a jaw which said its owner did not suffer fools gladly. He spoke, and his voice was crisp, and fully in control.

'You made good time here.'

'It wasn't difficult to find you. I know the area well.'

Briar remembered her brother's advice, and wasted no time herself in coming to the point. Crisping her own tone to match that of her client, she suggested briskly, 'Show me where the damage is, so that I can assess what needs to be done.'

'If my guess is correct, the damage is heading in our direction fast.'

He gestured towards a small boy, of about five or six years old, who came running at full speed around a corner of the house, shouting at the top of his voice,

'Vroom! Vroom! Watch me fly—I'm Concorde. Vroom!'

With his arms widespread to make aeroplane wings, and an intent look on his small face, that was almost a mirror image of the man's, the child veered away from them at an angle, and ran across the wide expanse of lawn, being Concorde for all he was worth.

'Has he been playing with matches?' Briar smiled. Mary had said there was no need of a plumber, so the damage could not be a flood.

'Nothing like that, unfortunately.'

'Unfortunately? What could be more unfortunate than a fire?'

'From the child's point of view, being abandoned.' Andrew Steel's glance registered Briar's shock, and he explained grimly, 'His mother has gone off on a hare-brained escapade to attend a theatrical audition, totally disregarding the fact that

I have to go abroad almost immediately on a business trip.'

It would take a brave woman to disregard Andrew Steel, Briar reflected, but carefully she kept her thoughts to herself, and hoped they did not show on her face as he went on, 'I urgently need a responsible person to come along with me, and take charge of the boy while I'm engaged on meetings and so on.'

Briar found her voice. 'You've made a mistake. We're not in the business of providing nannies.'

Something told her, uneasily, that Andrew Steel had made no mistake. That he was not in the business of making mistakes. That he had known exactly who it was he had telephoned, and what it was he wanted, and intended to get, from the Lycett Domestic Rescue Service. Heedless of her brother's instructions not to turn down the job, Briar argued,

'Why do you want to take him with you at all? Why don't you leave him here with someone until you get back?'

'The answer to your second question is, because I don't intend to. It's bad enough for his mother to go off without him, without me doing the same thing. I hope the new experiences of the trip out east will help to remove any ill effects caused by his mother's irresponsible action. Things like that can go deep with a young child, and I don't want him to grow up feeling permanently insecure.'

Things went deep with grown-ups too. Briar felt an urgent sympathy for the little boy. She knew exactly what it felt like to be abandoned.

Andrew Steel did not mince words when it came to criticising his wife's behaviour in front of a stranger, she thought, but, for all his grim exterior, he seemed to have a close rapport with his son. Briar's heart mourned. If only Philip had been like that! Andrew Steel's voice cut through a wave of pain.

'Your own advertisement answers your first question. You provide a domestic rescue service.'

'I know we do, but——'

'I should say that a small child who's been abandoned by his mother needs rescuing, wouldn't you?'

'Of course,' she agreed impatiently, 'but wait just a minute——'

'I haven't got time to wait. I have to be in Singapore by the end of the week. I assume you have a valid passport?' Taking her silence for agreement, he grasped her by the elbow and propelled her with him across the gravel towards the house.

'Come inside,' he ordered rather than invited, 'and we'll work out the details, and you can get acquainted with Tim.'

Briar felt as if she was being carried along on a whirlwind. Her definition of getting away from it all did not include jetting to the other side of the earth at a moment's notice, with a complete stranger and his young son, but . . .

'Don't refuse the job, no matter what it is.'

This was one story which would cap whatever it was Tony promised to tell her about the goats, Briar decided, and made a belated bid to assert herself.

'We don't set out to be a world service.'

Nerves gave her voice a cutting edge which she was sure her brother would not approve of, when speaking to a client, but Andrew Steel's expression registered no visible sign of damage, and he swept aside her objection with,

'Your advert says distance no object, so sit down, and tell me your name.'

He released her elbow, and Briar resisted the urge to rub the tingle that spread along the length of her arm from his touch. Electricity emanated from this man's fingertips, and she would have felt happier standing. Sitting down would put her at a disadvantage. Andrew Steel was tall, over six feet, she judged, and towered over her own very medium height, forcing her to look up at him, even when she was on her feet.

Her knees decided the issue for her. The trauma of walking away from her home, with all its memories of Lucy; of the nerve-stretching, traffic-filled motorway journey from London, and the untouched plate of cheese sandwiches, which wisdom dictated she should have eaten at least one of before she came out, suddenly caught up with her. Her knees folded, and she subsided suddenly on to the chair which her host pushed underneath her in the nick of time.

Andrew Steel selected a chair for himself, and positioned it opposite to her, giving Briar a brief space in which to look about her. The house was altered inside too, she noticed. Wide patio doors replaced the narrow french windows she remembered. They let in air and light on to a room of quiet elegance. She wondered if the tasteful furnishing was Andrew Steel's choice or his wife's. He broke into her thoughts with the reminder,

'Your name?'

'Lycett—Briar Lycett.'

'I know the Lycett part of it. The telephone operator told me.'

He was quick off the mark. Briar explained, 'The owner of the firm is my brother, Tony Lycett.'

'So, *Miss* Briar Lycett.' He made a quick deduction, and Briar let it go without comment. Her private life was nothing to do with a client. 'That's convenient,' Andrew Steel went on coolly, 'since it presumably means that you have no commitments.'

Briar wondered if it would have mattered to him if she had. She answered briefly, 'None.'

He nodded. 'I shall call you Briar. It suits you.' Interpreting her swift upwards glance, he added, 'You scratch.'

'Mr Steel, I——'

'Call me Drew,' he cut short her protest. 'Everybody does—it saves time.'

Time was not a commodity which Andrew Steel appeared to waste, but before Briar could retort he enquired, 'One more thing. Are you into the drugs habit?'

'Drugs?' Briar's voice rose in an indignant squeak. What next would this very determined client ask her? 'Of course not! Do I look as if I'd be such an idiot?'

'I didn't think you would, but I had to be sure.'

'Why . . . ?'

'Because drug-taking in Malaysia attracts the death penalty.'

'I haven't said I'm coming with you to Malaysia.'

Having just endured the stress of a divorce herself, the last thing she needed was to get involved in someone else's domestic conflict, particularly when the one partner was as forceful as this.

Andrew Steel said calmly, 'But you will, because your firm has agreed to accept me as a client.'

'No matter how way-out,' Tony had said. But surely not so way-out as this? Striving for calm, Briar tried again.

'Mr Steel, I——'

'*Drew.*'

'Drew, then.' Without thinking, she obeyed him, and immediately wanted to kick herself when she saw his eyes fire, scoring his victory. 'I shall have to talk this over with my brother,' she compromised. It was cowardly. She should have had the courage to say 'No,' for herself, and mean it. She added lamely, 'Tony might prefer to send along another member of staff. Someone who isn't already engaged on——'

She was going to add, 'on other contracts,' but Drew latched on to her words, and twisted their meaning to suit himself.

'*Is* Miss Briar Lycett engaged?' he asked softly. His eyes took in her ringless left hand, narrowed speculatively on the slight indent left by her wedding ring round its third finger, betraying the recent presence of the golden circlet which had turned into a manacle. 'I thought you said you had no commitments?'

'I'm not, and I haven't,' Briar answered tersely, despising herself for divulging personal information which was absolutely no concern of his. Hastily she digressed, before he had the opportunity to question her further, 'Your wife will want some say in who's going to look after your son, surely?'

'I haven't got a wife.'

Briar swallowed. This was getting worse by the minute. She felt out of her depth, and floundering, and lost her balance completely when he added,

'Or a son.'

'But . . . you said . . . I thought . . .'

'I didn't say that Tim was mine. I said he'd been dumped on me. And since you're obviously thinking the worst, I'll explain, for your own peace of mind.'

His eyes glinted, not with resentment of her suspicions, Briar saw with surprise, but with laughter. Laughing at her for the rush of colour which stained her throat and cheeks a delicate rose. Mocking the doubt and conjecture that flitted across her mobile features, allowing him to read her thoughts as easily as if they were on a printed page. Not caring what conclusions she came to, but telling her anyway, for her peace of mind.

Ruefully, Briar doubted if any woman would know peace of mind anywhere within radar distance of Andrew Steel. He was aggressively male. He exuded an aura of strength and dominance that flowed from him like radio waves, invisible, silent, but all the more potent because of that.

Potent, and dangerous. Briar stirred uneasily, grateful to Philip for the first time. Memories of her disastrous marriage should prove a powerful antidote to any future macho male, no matter how good-looking.

'Tim is my sister's son,' Drew informed her, watching her reaction.

Briar nodded, schooling her expression to show none. 'That explains the likeness.' She wondered if there was a father in the offing, but she did not dare to ask. It would be treading in a minefield to broach the subject, and Drew did not strike her as a person who would welcome prying, even though he had not scrupled to do some of his own.

'The boy has inherited the family colouring. My sister and I are very much alike in looks.'

'Not in character?'

'Definitely not in character. Elizabeth is impulsive, and given to delusions about her acting abilities. She's the leading light in her local amateur dramatic society—hence the audition.'

'She must have some talent, if she's in the local drama group.'

'She has, but that doesn't excuse her walking out on her child. Or for leaving me to cope with the consequences.'

Which of the two sins took precedence with Drew? Briar wondered. Reluctantly conceding a point, she decided that the interests of the child would win hands down with his uncle, although she doubted if a grown-up would merit such consideration in his eyes.

'Vroom! Vrooooom!'

'It looks as if Concorde's coming back,' Drew remarked, and raised his voice. 'Tim, touch down a minute, will you, and come and meet Briar? She's coming out to Singapore with us,' he announced, as the child ran obediently through the patio doors and skidded to a halt beside his uncle's chair.

'I didn't say I——' Briar protested.

Drew's look cut her short. It sliced across the space between them, and dared her to go any further. It said, Don't *you* walk out on him too, and warned her that she, and her brother's firm, would answer to him for the consequences if she did. Briar began to feel sorry for his sister when the two met again.

She felt sorry for herself as well. Tony had bailed her out when she most needed help. Much more, she suspected, than her brother did, but he was too generous to say so. How could she let him down now? And if she did, would Andrew Steel sue for breach of contract? She had only the vaguest notion of what constituted a legally binding agreement.

Her intuition about people was on firmer ground, however. It warned her clearly that Andrew Steel would make a good friend but a bad enemy. It would be unthinkable for her to put Tony's future plans for expansion at risk.

Tim's smile distracted her. He had an open, friendly grin, which warmed some of the ice inside her. Would Drew's smile be just as warm? And what would it feel like to be on the receiving end of it? Hastily Briar put a brake on her thoughts and forced herself to concentrate on what Tim was saying.

'Uncle Drew says we're going to fly—not on Concorde, but in a plane that will be almost as big. Do you like flying, Briar?'

'Mmm, I love it.'

'So do I. Mummy doesn't though. She says the bumps make her feel sick. I'm staying with Uncle Drew until she comes back from her audition.'

Briar said carefully, 'You'll feel very proud of her if she gets the part, won't you?'

In spite of Drew's poor opinion of his sister's talents, the unknown Elizabeth might have more ability than her brother gave her credit for, and it was as well to prepare Tim for having to face the possibility that his mother might be accepted for the part. If she was, it could take her away from home, and him, for some considerable time, if the play was successful.

Her sidelong glance registered Drew's thunderous scowl at her temerity, but she steeled herself to ignore it. It would not help either him or his nephew if he refused to face facts. She beamed her attention on to Tim, and her heart twisted at the child's suddenly woebegone expression, which said plainly enough that it would be a personal disaster to him if his mother succeeded. Briar suggested gently,

'When you're in Singapore, it would be nice if you kept a diary of all the things you see and do. You'll be able to show it to your mummy then, when you get home. You'll have lots of things to tell each other, won't you?'

The child's face brightened. 'I've never kept a diary before. Will you help me? I'm learning to do joined-up writing at school, but I'm not very good at it yet.'

'Yes, of course I'll help you. We'll do it together.'

She had committed herself! Briar could have bitten her tongue for speaking the words. Without intending to do anything of the kind, she had walked straight into the trap which Drew had cunningly set for her, using the child as bait. She felt the door close behind her with an almost audible clang, and Drew's smile of satisfaction turned the key in the lock, effectively preventing her escape.

Anger at Drew for his cynical manipulation, against herself for falling such an easy prey, boiled up inside her, but before she could give it utterance Drew said smoothly,

'When you go out, Tim, pull the side curtain along a bit, will you? The sun's getting in Briar's eyes.'

Bring the curtains back with you...

Tension suddenly exploded in a helpless giggle, and Drew slanted an enquiring glance in her direction.

'What's funny?'

'The curtains,' Briar gurgled. 'Tony told me to b-bring back the c-curtains with me.'

Tony echoed her laughter when she reported back to her brother an hour later, over another pot of tea and the now sadly curled cheese sandwiches. If his sister's laughter held a note of hysteria, he did not seem to notice.

'That's great, Briar,' he exulted. 'It's just the break I've been looking for.'

'Break? I don't see——'

'Into the commercial side of the business, of course. Didn't you know? Andrew Steel is head of the Steel Engineering Corporation—they're the biggest thing in civil engineering in the whole of the Midlands. Since he took over as chairman, after his father retired, he's worked day and night to bring the firm into the twentieth century. And *how* he's succeeded!' His voice held awed respect. 'They were quite a small outfit, to start with. Now they're international. If we can manage to satisfy them, we'll be made in the commercial field. After only half a day on our payroll, you've succeeded in netting the fish I've been angling for for ages,' he congratulated her.

'You land him, then,' Briar mumbled through a mouthful of cheese sandwich. 'I feel more inclined to throw him back into the water.'

'You can't turn him down, Briar!' Tony's look was anguished. 'We haven't got anyone else suitable on our staff to send in your place, and we might never get such an opportunity again.'

She could not turn Tony down, and there lay the crunch. The knowledge wiped the smile from Briar's face, and made the much-needed sandwich suddenly difficult to swallow. Tony's glee was misplaced so far as she was concerned. Having hooked his fish for him, she felt in grave danger—her catch might turn and swallow her whole.

CHAPTER TWO

SINGAPORE was a revelation to Briar, and the journey there even more so.

After that first meeting with Andrew Steel, things happened with lightning speed, and she hardly had time to catch her breath before she found herself in the plane, and heading into the sunrise. Drew whiled away some of the long flight time for them by explaining the nature of his mission.

'We're building a string of landing strips for light aircraft on all the small islands from Malaysia, right across to the northern tip of Australia.'

'It sounds a huge project!' Briar exclaimed, and thought, Nothing would be too big for this man to achieve, if he so desired. Out loud she commented, 'It must cut across a lot of political boundaries.'

'It does. But the various governments have got together to see it through. They've recognised the need for better communication between the people who live on these very small islands. The oil companies, too, have got in on the act. They've been very generous with funding, and with the loan of equipment, which has been an enormous help.'

'I thought there was a good sprinkling of airports out there already, serving the tourist trade?'

'There are airports on most of the larger islands—they're well enough served. But the small islands, and there are an awful lot of them, are little more than the tips of extinct volcanoes. They're mountainous, and covered with thick jungle. They're only sparsely populated, but if someone in one the jungle villages becomes seriously ill, or injured, it's often too late by the time they're able to reach the nearest hospital on the mainland. A landing strip would bring immediate help.'

'A sort of flying doctor service?' Briar was interested in spite of herself.

'More or less, although it will have other uses as well.'

'Such as?'

'It will bring in supplies of essentials to the remote villages, and take out the villagers' craft work for sale on the coast. It will help to boost the standard of living on the islands, and, they hope, stop the drain of the young people away from their home lands. They have much higher aspirations than their parents had. If a better way of life can be brought to them, instead of them having to leave to go in search of it, it may prevent the island life from dying.'

Briar looked at Drew curiously. His profession stamped him as a practical man. She had discovered that he could be ruthless in getting his own way. She had not realised that he was a visionary as well.

He went on, 'Progress meetings are held frequently, along with site inspections, which is what's taking me out there on this trip. This is the island we're working on at the moment.'

He snapped open his briefcase and produced a map on which blue and green dots figured prominently. Tim reached across and traced the dots with a curious finger.

'What are they all for, Uncle Drew?'

'The blue dots are the landing strips we've already built. The red dot is the one we're building at the moment, and the green dots are the ones we still have to do.' Drew held out the map to his nephew. 'You can clip this in the front of your diary, if you like, to start it off.'

In the departure lounge at the airport, Drew had urged Briar, 'Plug that diary for all it's worth. It was a brilliant idea of yours. Tim's full of it. He can't wait to start writing up the events of his first day, to show to his mother when he gets back home.'

Briar felt an absurd uprush of pleasure at the praise. She jeered at herself, but she could not help it. It was such a sharp contrast to Philip's constant carping after their child was born. She had tried to excuse him, on the grounds that it probably stemmed from jealousy of the baby. With hindsight, she realised that it was the defence of a weak character, needing to put somebody else down, in order to feed his own ego.

'Isn't my diary nice, Briar? Uncle Drew gave it to me.' Tim tugged a bright scarlet loose-leaf binder from his cabin baggage, and held it up for Briar's inspection. 'I've put my name on the first page,' he showed her proudly.

Briar approved, 'You've done it beautifully.' The large, round, but commendably neat joined-up writing announced, 'Timothy Grainger'. Grainger, not Steel. So Elizabeth must have a husband in the background, somewhere, either present or ex. She pulled her mind back to what Tim was telling her.

'Look, the pages are all punched at the side. That means I can have some more to put in the binder when I've finished these up.'

'If you're thinking of using up more than those, you'd better title the binder Volume One. You'll probably need three more to go with it, one for each week you're away.'

Four weeks. Briar's heart misgave her. To get through them safely she was going to need the distraction of the diary as much as Tim. The close daily contact with Drew, which looking after his nephew would necessarily involve, posed a challenge which she felt barely equal to, so soon after Philip. She hoped Drew's business meetings would keep him fully occupied for most of the time, to leave her in the far less demanding company of the child.

Tim slept for a good part of the flight. Tired out by excitement, he dropped into the sound, dreamless slumber of childhood, and Briar envied him the ability. She felt too strung-up herself to rest, and, lacking Tim's bright chatter to act as a buffer between herself and Drew, she felt tension begin to mount inside her.

To counteract it, she took refuge in the bundle of magazines which Tony had picked up from the local paper shop the evening before, to help speed her journey. His choice was haphazard. They were the popular women's weeklies, not much to her taste, but, rather than hurt her brother's feelings, she'd added them to her luggage, and leafed through them now in a desultory fashion.

She wrinkled her nose at the predictable letters ·on the back page, glanced without interest at a diet recipe which her too slender figure did not need anyway, and took in the eye-catching title of an article exhorting married women to 'Find fulfilment in a career outside home.'

Drew's snort of disgust arrested her reading.

'Such rubbish!' His forefinger stabbed at the page as if it was a personal affront. 'Articles like that cause most of the trouble,' he growled.

'It's only a guide on how to cope with a career as well as running a home and family,' Briar said mildly.

'Exactly. It sets out to make women feel inadequate and dissatisfied, if they remain at home to bring up a family. Fulfilment!' he snorted. 'Having children should be fulfilment enough for any woman. It's a career in itself, only the silly creatures either can't or won't see it.'

If only she had had the opportunity to remain at home to look after Lucy! The hurt of it lay like a leaden weight on Briar's heart, as Drew swept on, 'Articles like that ought to be banned.'

His wholesale condemnation nettled Briar. How typically, arrogantly male! He might have steered his firm into the twentieth century, but his view on women was positively mid-Victorian. Doubtless his opinion was coloured by his sister's feckless behaviour, but that did not give him the right to class all women the same.

The sturdy spirit that drove Briar up the ladder of her own career, to which she would probably have returned when Lucy was of school age, gave her the courage to flash back,

'Women aren't just childbearing machines. They've got minds of their own as well.'

'So have children. They've got minds that can be bruised and warped by the callous behaviour of adults.' Drew's voice was vibrant with anger, although he kept it low, mindful of the child sleeping between them. 'Girls should get their priorities sorted out before they get married. No man wants a weekend wife.'

This was too much! Thoroughly roused now, Briar declared vigorously, 'So should the men get their priorities right! Children have got fathers as well as mothers. It isn't always the women who are to blame. What of the men who opt out, the moment they're put to the slightest inconvenience by the babies they themselves have fathered?'

She was unconscious of the depth of bitterness in her voice, which earned her a searching look from Drew, but all he said was, 'I was referring to Elizabeth.'

His qualification did nothing to appease Briar. All the hurt and humiliation she had endured at Philip's hands spilled out of her in justification of her own sex.

'You condemn your sister—but what about her husband? Where does Tim's father fit into the scene?'

Immediately she spoke, she wished her words unsaid. What if Elizabeth was a widow? She felt a flood of relief when Drew replied,

'Robert is head of our research team. He has to spend a lot of time away from home. At the moment he's abroad.'

'That doesn't excuse him neglecting his wife and child. You pour scorn on weekend wives, but what about weekend husbands? Children need both parents to have a hand in their upbringing, not just the one. The men need to get their priorities right, as well as their wives.'

'*Touché*! Briar keeps her thorns well sharpened,' Drew taunted, and deepened the red flags of indignation that rode her cheeks. Her colour receded swiftly when he added, 'It might jolt Elizabeth into reassessing her priorities, when she returns to the Paddocks and finds the foal is missing.'

Briar stared at him, stunned. 'Do you mean you haven't let her know where you're taking Tim?'

She did not need Drew's curt nod of confirmation to give her his answer. His look of steely determination answered for him, and she burst out, aghast, 'But—but that's kidnapping!' The realisation that she too was involved hit her like a thunderbolt. 'I won't be a party to it,' she gasped.

'You *are* a party to it, whether you like it or not.'

He was unbelievable. Outrageous. What he had done was so cruel. The man acted as if he was a law unto himself. The fact that other, more traditional laws might not recognise this did not seem to occur to him. It occurred to Briar, however, and the possible penalties made her quail. The ruthless manner in which he had implicated her was frightening.

'I don't like it, not one little bit,' she declared forcefully. 'You have no right to make me an accessory! I said I won't be a party to it, and I mean just that. The very moment we reach Singapore, I'm going to turn right round and go back home on the next plane!'

'Mummy?' The sleepy whimper from the seat next to her cut Briar short. Hastily corking up her indignation, she beamed her attention on Tim, and the sight of his woebegone face wrenched at her .

In that most vulnerable of moments, between sleeping and waking, before full consciousness drew down the mask that hid the innermost feelings from the unfeeling world, the full depth of the child's unhappiness and insecurity lay naked on Tim's small, crumpled features for the grown-ups to see. Disarmed, Briar crooned softly,

'It's Briar, darling. Wake up—we're nearly at Singapore.'

She swallowed an uncomfortable lump in her throat, and reached down to fold the little boy in her arms and hold him close for a moment or two until he felt strong enough to cope for himself once more, and knew quick surprise that, in comforting Tim, a small measure of comfort seeped back to warm her too. Perhaps it was the feeling of having her arms full again, that had for too long been as empty as her heart.

As she felt Tim's urgent return clasp, she knew that she could not walk out on him as well, and be responsible for bringing that look back to his face for a second time, perhaps permanently.

She dared not look at Drew. He had won, as he fully intended to, and she had no desire to witness the triumph which must ride his expression, as surely as misery rode Tim's.

'Let's notice as many things as we can, to write about in your diary,' she distracted the child, and had Tim chattering happily again by the time they emerged into the bustle of the mini-city that was Singapore's international airport. Drew helped her efforts along as they cleared Customs, by picking up a handful of tourist leaflets from a nearby rack and handing them to his nephew with the promise,

'These are only a few of the places we'll go to see while we're here. The leaflets will help you to remember all the details you need, to put in your diary afterwards.'

'Still with us?' he taunted Briar softly as he helped her into a taxi beside Tim, and she gritted her teeth on the retort which Drew was maddeningly aware she would not utter in front of the child, but fascination quickly outbid vexation as they sped towards the city, and she exclaimed,

'I didn't expect Singapore to be so...so...'

'Green?' Drew suggested, glancing appreciatively at the brilliant flowerbeds and the meticulously barbered lawns that flanked the busy main road. 'It's the climate. As it's warm and humid, everything grows easily. Perfect if you're interested in gardening.'

Was Drew interested in gardening?

Briar did not know. In fact, she knew almost nothing about what interested this man, except for his work, and the welfare of his young nephew. Beyond that, he was a closed book. What might she read on the pages in the weeks that lay ahead? The possibilities both intrigued and disturbed her, and hastily she steered her thoughts back to their previous, less dangerous channels.

'Everywhere looks so clean! I haven't seen a scrap of litter anywhere since we landed.'

'That's because the authorities here clamp down hard on litter-louts. The same applies to jay-walkers. So don't be tempted to try to dash across the road among the traffic, or to drop so much as a sweet wrapping, or you'll be fined on the spot. And if you are, you'll pay out of your own pocket money, to teach you a lesson,' Drew warned them jointly.

Briar and Tim both laughed, as they were meant to, but the thought that tracked across Briar's mind took the brightness from her smile. If the authorities here punished jay-walkers and litter-droppers so severely, what would they do to people who absconded with other people's children?

'Take it easy for the next couple of days,' Drew advised her the next morning. 'Give yourself time to become acclimatised, and to get over any feelings of jet lag.'

He did not seem to suffer from it himself. He appeared early, dressed in a tracksuit and trainers, as if he had already been out on a jogging stint. Briar was in the process of preparing Tim's breakfast, squeezing fresh orange juice, and shaking out cornflakes, in the tiny kitchenette which was attached to the luxurious executive suite in the central hotel which had widened her eyes when they took possession the evening before.

'Coffee's ready!' she called out automatically, and regretted her impulse a moment later when Drew checked his stride towards his room and joined her in the kitchenette instead.

'It smells good,' he sniffed appreciatively.

The kitchenette was not meant to hold two people. Drew's broad-shouldered, six-foot-plus frame filled it to capacity, and Briar hastily busied herself at the percolator as an antidote to his disturbing closeness, and urged, 'Let's take it to the dining area. It's a bit cramped in here.'

It was claustrophobic, and the reason was more Drew himself than the smallness of the kitchenette. How different he looked, dressed in casuals. Until now Briar had only seen him in formal business attire, the impeccably tailored, dark-suited badge of office that went with his position as head of his firm. In sports clothes, he looked younger, more relaxed, and infinitely more approachable.

He remarked with a boyish grin, that closely resembled Tim's, 'I couldn't have timed my return better. Is Tim awake yet?'

'No. I let him sleep on this morning. I'll give him his breakfast as soon as he wakes up.'

'Have you had yours?'

'Not yet. I was just going to pop a piece of bread in the toaster.'

'Make that two pieces, and I'll have mine with you.'

The two pieces of bread flipped up in the toaster, done to a turn, and to her dismay, Briar felt her heart imitate their acrobatics. There was a disconcerting intimacy about munching buttered toast for breakfast with Drew that was too much like being back at the flat with Philip. And yet so very unlike. Drew was fresh and alert and willing to talk. Philip had been monosyllabic and moody first thing in the morning.

'I'm a night person,' he had excused his pettish early morning temper.

Briar did not need him to remind her of that. She hid a grimace in an extra hard bite on her toast, as if by so abusing the bread she could destroy the memory.

Drew enquired, 'Is your crust burnt? Mine seems to be all right.'

He was too noticing by half! Briar wondered what his reaction would be if he could know her thoughts. She felt her ready colour rise, and mumbled through a mouthful of toast,

'It's a bit chippy, that's all. I'd bitten off more than I could chew.'

Had she done exactly that with this too observant client? Should she have taken Drew's own advice, and given herself more time to become acclimatised, instead of taking on the world again before she was ready? She could scarcely have chosen a more drastic remedy for her ills, and she wondered uneasily if the cure might turn out to be worse than the ills themselves.

She hoped her relief did not show on her face when Drew told her, 'I shall be out at progress meetings most of today and tomorrow. After that, I shall have more spare time to take Tim out and about, and help to find things to fill in his diary. Meantime, I rely on you to keep him fully occupied, and stop him from brooding about his mother.'

'I'll do my best,' Briar promised, and meant it.

Drew nodded. 'There's an excellent swimming-pool at the rear of the hotel, which might help if you get stuck for ideas. Tim likes the water. Do you swim?'

'Yes, but I haven't brought a costume away with me. I didn't notice one in Tim's luggage either, when I unpacked his case last night.'

'He didn't bring much with him to the Paddocks. He and Elizabeth were only going to stay for a couple of nights, and then Robert was due to collect them for a weekend together on the coast, before he went abroad. But a crisis cropped up in the lab, and he had to cancel at the last minute.'

How many crises had cropped up, and how many promises had been broken, to finally cause Elizabeth to crack and run? Briar wondered, but carefully she refrained from asking. She still smarted from her argument with Drew on the plane. It had been brief but fierce, and she did not relish the prospect of a return bout. Let him hold whatever chauvinistic views he liked as regarded a woman's role. Once her contracted month was up, Drew and his opinions would no longer matter to her.

Carefully skating on to firmer ice, she said, 'I noticed some big stores just before the taxi dropped us off here last night. I'm sure I could get Tim a pair of swimming-trunks from one of them.'

'Don't stint, get him a decent pair. In fact, I want you to kit him out completely. He's got nothing with him that's really suitable for the heat and the humidity over here. Five or six cotton outfits should be enough. The hotel has a same-day laundry service.'

Five or six outfits! Briar's eyebrows rose. Drew was a man who thought big, even in everyday matters. She wondered if he realised how much half a dozen outfits for a small boy would cost him. Before she could comment, he went on,

'Don't forget to add a couple of woollies to your shopping list—the air-conditioning in these hotels can become quite arctic at times. He'll need something to play with as well. I didn't bring any of his toys along, but there's a big toy store fairly close. Oh, and buy a swimsuit for yourself as well. I'll pay.'

'There's no need.' Pride brought a protesting flush to Briar's cheeks.

'There's every need. I won't allow you to be out of pocket on my behalf. Regard it as equipment for the job,' he told her firmly, and added before she could argue further,

'When you're ready to go out, take this down to the reception desk, and they'll change it for the necessary currency. If it doesn't cover everything you need, let me know, and I'll top it up.'

Briar accepted the folded banknotes from his fingers, and felt her own tingle as their tips touched briefly before Drew released the paper. She said hurriedly, 'I'll try to find the store we passed yesterday.'

'There are masses of shops and stores within easy walking distance,' he told her. 'You'll be spoiled for choice. We're right in the middle of Orchard Road here—it's the main shopping area of the city. Now I must go. Don't wait up for me, I don't know what time I'll be back.'

He popped his head round the door of Tim's room, and assured the now sleepily rousing boy, 'Briar will be with you all the time until I get back.' On his way to the door he threw over his shoulder to Briar, 'By the way, if you take a taxi, don't make the mistake of tipping the driver. It isn't done out here.' And then he was gone.

Tim was inclined to be querulous, the weariness of the long flight of the day before still with him. To distract him, Briar enlarged on the attractions of the hotel swimming-pool, and the coming shopping trip.

It reminded her of the banknotes she still held clutched in her fingers, and while Tim was engaged with his orange juice and cornflakes, she flattened them out. The total amount made her blink.

Drew not only thought big, he spent big as well. There was enough here to purchase a dozen outfits, and a nursery full of toys. Nevertheless, Briar shopped with care. For all she knew, Drew might be testing her, and she had no intention of confirming his opinion of all women as being feckless and irresponsible.

For Tim, she bought two nicely made cotton suits for best, three pairs of bright cotton shorts, and half a dozen mix-and-match tops to go with them, which would ensure her charge would remain in mint condition for the rest of the month.

Tim chose his swimming-trunks himself, bright scarlet, with a smart white stripe down the sides, and Briar purchased a cover-up honey-coloured costume for herself, with a neat rubber cap to match, both carefully in a middle-of-the-range price so that Drew should not be able to accuse her of extravagance at his expense.

There were plenty of designer boutiques, with their window displays ominously unpriced, rubbing shoulders with international stores, and individual shops of good but reasonably priced articles, which Briar promised herself she would browse among if she had the opportunity before she returned home.

Singapore was a shopper's paradise, if one had the money to spend, but she was mindful that most of the currency in her purse was not her own, and she passed them by and headed purposefully for the toy store.

Its offerings rivalled the famous London emporium, and she and Tim spent a blissful hour exploring its tempting arcades. Briar bought the child a ball with her own money, unable to resist the temptation to spoil him a little. The ball was big, and brightly coloured, lightweight enough to play with in the swimming-pool, and large enough to serve as a kicking ball outside.

Tim selected his own colouring book and crayons, and some reading matter which surprised Briar by its advanced standard, and he surprised her still more by requesting in a small voice, just as they were getting ready to leave the store, 'Can I have a teddy to take back with me, please?'

His expression was tight, his eyes desperate pools of entreaty, begging Briar not to laugh at him. Pity flooded her. He wanted something to cuddle. Something that would always be there when he wanted it, that did not break promises, or disappear on missions of more importance than himself.

She answered him casually, 'I saw some gorgeous teddies just inside the door as we came in. I'd love one myself, only I thought you might laugh at me if I said so.'

Relief chased away the tightness, and Tim promised her gravely, 'I won't laugh. You can share my teddy, if you like.'

Sharing would forge a link between them, and at the moment Tim was desperately in need of links that did not break under pressure. Briar nodded. 'I'd like that. Which one shall we have?'

Tim chose one with soft brown fur and a wise-looking face, and Briar smiled at the assistant, who was about to add the toy to their other purchases for dispatch to the hotel.

'We'll take him with us, I think.'

They took it in turns to carry the bear as they strolled slowly back along the broad, tiled sidewalks, stopping on the way for an ice-cream sundae for Tim and a coffee for Briar.

Later, the bear sat at the hotel poolside, waiting for its young owner while they tried out their new swimming-costumes, and the toy was firmly clasped in the crook of Tim's arm when Briar finally tucked him up in bed for the night.

She ruffled the brown fur, kissed Tim, 'Sleep tight, poppet,' and she knew from the sound of the boy's quiet breathing that he was already half asleep before she reached the door. She left it slightly ajar in case he might wake up and want her, and settled at the well-stocked writing-table in the sitting-room to pen a progress report to Tony.

In it she poured out her concern at Drew's high-handed action in carrying off his sister's child without letting the mother know where he had gone, and she felt better as she sealed and stamped the envelope and popped it into the hotel posting-box for airmail correspondence. It should be in Tony's hands within a couple of days, and then if trouble did arise she could rely on her brother to support her.

With her mind more at ease, she stretched her cramped arms, revelling in the unaccustomed luxury of having nothing to do. She wished she had bought some reading matter for herself as well as for Tim.

The television did not appeal to her, and she did not want to read the women's magazines which had caused such a sharp exchange between herself and Drew on the plane.

He had still not put in an appearance; presumably he was dining out. Briar did not know whether to wish he would turn up, or to be glad that he did not. His company was challenging, abrasive, and profoundly disturbing by turns, but the alternative left her to fall back on her own thoughts, with all the memories they brought with them, and she did not relish those either.

To keep them at bay, she picked up the glossy hotel brochure that lay aslant the writing-table top. The hotel was one of a large international chain, and the facilities it offered to the wealthy traveller were the last word in luxury. The roomy suite which Drew had engaged for them on the first floor consisted of two large bedrooms, with a dressing-room opening off the one, which had been turned into a bedroom for Tim, giving Briar trouble -free access to the child at night.

True, the kitchenette was minute, but with a speedy twenty-four-hour room service it was a mere token utility, and the sitting-room was large and airy, with picture windows overlooking the hotel gardens which, in keeping with what she had seen so far of the rest of the city, were beautifully maintained.

The list of facilities in the brochure seemed endless, but it was the final offering that riveted Briar's attention. It stipulated, 'Spouse accommodated free of charge in all executive suites.'

Briar felt herself go hot, then cold. Had Drew booked her in as his spouse? After the way he had virtually abducted Tim, she would not put anything past him.

Was she, in the eyes of the hotel staff, Mrs Steel? She burned to know, and shrank from finding out. Since she had just shed her married status, the possibility of having it reconferred against her will by a domineering male, to whom she was in no way attached, was galling in the extreme.

She tried to remember how the smiling waiter had addressed her when he had answered her request for room service with a delicious evening meal for herself and Tim, but the man had been a charming Chinese, with a lisping accent, and she could easily have mistaken Mrs for Miss. She had had no reason to take any special notice at the time.

She recalled now, however, that it had been Drew who signed the hotel register. At his suggestion, Briar had taken the travel-weary child straight up to the suite, leaving the formalities of arrival to Drew. Exactly as a wife would have done. How easily he had managed to manipulate her, so that she had no opportunity to see the hotel register.

Too late, she wished she had waited, and signed her own name. It would look odd if she asked to inspect the book now.

Briar was thoughtful as she prepared for bed. Another, and equally disturbing aspect of Drew's probable booking-in rose to confront her. Tim resembled his uncle in looks sufficiently for him to pass as Drew's child.

Had Drew signed them in as Mr and Mrs Steel and son, in order to throw a red herring across Elizabeth's trail if she should return to the Paddocks in the meantime, and attempt to trace the whereabouts of her child?

CHAPTER THREE

BRIAR and Tim were in the swimming-pool, playing with the new ball, when Drew returned to the hotel the next afternoon.

She had seen him only briefly that morning, when he returned from jogging, and shared coffee and toast with her as before, but the cosy intimacy of the previous meal was gone, because Tim was up and dressed this morning, and ate his breakfast with them.

Her attempt to give Drew back the change, and a detailed account of her shopping the day before, brought his brows together in a frown, and earned her the rebuke, 'If I wanted you to account for every dollar, I'd have said so.'

At his insistence, she retained the change, but she still kept a meticulous account of what she spent when she took Tim out to lunch, and when she purchased some reading matter for herself she used her own money.

The attraction of the swimming-pool enticed them, as the heat increased during the afternoon, and a game of toss the ball was in full spate when Drew slipped into the pool to join them.

Briar did not see him arrive. The sudden lighting up of Tim's face should have warned her, but she was so intent on fielding a particularly high throw that she did not notice. With her head upraised, and her arms stretched up to catch the flighting ball, she looked like a slender golden nymph outlined against the glistening water, coloured a deep green by the reflection of the pool tiles.

The ball sailed over her head, she turned to swim after it, and came face to face with Drew. He held the ball aloft between the palms of his hands, and his eyes were alight with laughter as he dangled it tantalisingly above her head.

'Your costume suits you,' he approved, and the added glint in his eyes could have been laughter or it could have been something else, and the uncertainty deepened the colour that stained Briar's throat and cheeks.

'Catch, Tim!' Drew called out, and tossed the ball, again over Briar's head, and quick as a flash she turned and dived after it, using the move as an excuse to hide her burning face, which grew no cooler as she carried with her under water a disturbing picture of a hard, suntanned body, mounting powerful shoulders, and a tight waist that carried not a surplus ounce of flesh.

Within seconds Drew was beside her, stroking down through the water with a nonchalant ease that told her she had no hope of outdistancing his superior strength. A feeling of irrational fear gripped her, and she urged her arms to the limit of her strength to draw away from him, to no avail, and at last her depleted lungs forced her upwards.

She did not know quite how it happened, but when she broke the surface, it was within the wide-spread circle of Drew's arms. His one hand held the ball, which he promptly tossed to Tim, sending the boy swimming eagerly to the far side of the pool, and then the circle closed, and Briar found herself trapped inside it.

'Mermaids are supposed to have long golden hair,' Drew told her gravely, and with one slender index finger he prised up the rubber cap and tipped it back off her head, leaving her brown curls free to tumble across her forehead, while, with his other hand firm against her back, he pulled her towards him, the better to press his lips down hard on her own.

Briar jerked away from his kiss as if she had been stung, and her eyes were stormy pools of shock. No man had touched her since Philip, whose touch had not always been gentle, and after the divorce she had promised herself no man should have the opportunity again. She would keep men at a distance, preferably a long distance, from now on, and that included Drew. She had provided the ball for a plaything, not herself.

She should have known that Drew was a man who provided his own opportunities.

'Loose me!' she hissed at him furiously. 'Tim's coming back!'

'Catch, Briar!' the little boy called out. 'Let her have a turn, Uncle Drew.'

Tim tossed, and Briar caught, and the iron circle parted to allow her to go free. Seizing the opportunity, she swam quickly away from Drew, forgetting her rubber cap until Tim shouted,

'Your hair's getting wet, Briar. Did your cap come off?'

'Yes—the strap's a bit loose. I'll go back to my room and adjust it. Stay with your uncle until I come back.'

She had no intention of coming back. She grabbed her floating headgear and hauled herself up the pool steps on legs that felt suddenly unsure of themselves. As she ran along the poolside, she was confusedly conscious of Drew's mocking glance following her, appreciating the view afforded by her clinging wet costume, aware that she was running not so much to her room as away from him.

She passed the lounger where Tim's teddy bear sat on guard over their towels, and snatched up one. Not waiting to see if it was her own, she flung it across her shoulders, grateful for the sheltering folds of cloth, and longed to shut her ears against the low, derisive laugh that followed her flight.

To Briar's relief, a business meeting, followed by a working dinner, removed Drew from her orbit for the rest of that day, and allowed her time to regain her poise before she met up with him again, but the prospect of the weekend to come, when he would be free to escort Tim and herself on the promised sightseeing tour, caused her second night in Singapore to be as restless as her first.

Her disturbed sleep was not helped by wondering whether Elizabeth had yet managed to track down Tim's whereabouts. Briar gave a small shiver of apprehension. If the boy's mother chose to be vindictive, the outings to which Tim was so eagerly looking forward could end, in the time-honoured phrase, with Drew and herself, 'helping the police with their inquiries.'

No such misgivings seemed to trouble Drew, however. At breakfast the next morning, he suggested to Tim, 'Let's find something different to fill your diary today. We'll start with a trishaw ride through Chinatown, then take the day from there.'

It was pure tourist, colourful, noisy, and larger than life, and Tim enjoyed himself hugely. Briar put her unease to one side and entered into the spirit of the thing in order to encourage her charge, and soon found that she was enjoying herself as much as the child.

Drew seemed to have an encyclopaedic knowledge of Singapore. He appeared to know by instinct the things that would most interest them, and guided them from one to another at a leisurely pace that ensured that neither of his companions grew either physically or mentally weary.

'We'll walk from here,' he decided, judging to a nicety when Tim's lively energy needed release from the novelty of the trishaw, and rewarded the driver's hard work with a generosity which brought a pleased grin to that worthy's face. That done, he turned to lift Tim safely down beside him then reached up for Briar.

'I can manage,' she began hurriedly, but for all the notice Drew took she might not have spoken. He reached up into the wicker vehicle, and his hands were a hard clamp around her waist. Briar gave a gasp as she felt herself lifted bodily upwards, as easily as if she weighed no more than Tim, and then she was placed carefully down on to terra firma beside Drew, so close beside him that his eyes looked straight down into her startled face.

They fired, and Briar knew a moment of pure panic as she stood transfixed, gazing up at him. Her heart began to pound, then the blaze died, abruptly extinguished as if Drew had reached out

and switched off a light, and he released her, punc-
tilious in his regard for the local dislike of public
display.

Would he have released her if they had been
alone? Relief at being freed battled with confusion
in Briar's mind, leaving her uncertain if she had
really seen the fire in his eyes, or whether it was a
mere figment of her imagination, reacting to the
episode in the swimming-pool the day before.

She would have to be on her guard, against
herself as much as against Drew. In spite of her
vow to remain aloof, and the lesson of Philip to
reinforce it, she was more vulnerable than she had
believed herself to be.

Tim was the perfect antidote. He walked between them, swinging on a hand of each, a small,
energetic link, who put introspection to flight, and
demanded that they wonder with him at the fierce
roof-top dragons that crouched on top of the
temples, and laugh at the colourful and earsplit-
tingly noisy street opera, performed purely for the
benefit of tourists, but enjoyed just as much by the
equally noisy hawkers calling their wares nearby.

They gazed in admiration at a display of cleverly
made paper models of every conceivable worldly
luxury, while the scent of incense wafted round
them from a small shopfront shrine, and the click
of mah-jong tiles from the shadowy interior beat
time to the leisurely pace of their stroll. Tim gazed
wistfully at one particularly striking paper model
of a car.

'It's a beaut!' he breathed ungrammatically.

'Those models are funeral offerings for a dead
person to use in the next world,' Drew diffused his

admiration. 'They're meant to be burned, not played with.'

He made up for the boy's disappointment soon afterwards by purchasing a brightly painted kite, and promising, 'We'll fly it in the park tomorrow.'

They paused to watch a Chinese calligrapher at work on his makeshift writing table, propped up against the kerb, and Drew spoke to the man in his own language. The scribe nodded, and carefully began to paint on a long, narrow piece of parchment.

When it was finished, he exchanged it with Drew for some coins, and the boy's uncle handed it over with the remark, 'This will make a nice bookmark for your diary.'

'What does it say?' Tim frowned down at the intricate characters.

'It's an ancient Chinese proverb.' Drew translated loosely, in deference to the boy's tender years. 'In effect, it says that to be kind is better than to be clever.'

Would that others had taken the same advice, principally Philip, Briar thought with a flash of bitterness, as Tim nodded, and begged, 'Can Briar have one too?'

'No, Tim, you mustn't ask for me,' Briar protested, embarrassed, but Drew agreed readily enough.

'Briar shall have one too,' he said, and spoke at greater length to the calligrapher.

Her own piece of parchment was of a size that could be fitted into a small frame. It held three lines of beautifully formed characters, and Briar raised her face to Drew as she took it from his hand.

'Thank you. It's beautiful.'

Suddenly her tongue seemed to stick. She had been about to ask, as Tim had done, what the writing said, but for some reason the words refused to come. Drew's eyes rested on her face, registering her difficulty, challenging her to ask him, and she felt her colour come and go.

Then Tim saved her by piping up, 'What does Briar's say, Uncle Drew? Is hers a proverb too?'

'No. It's a kind of—promise.'

Strangely, Drew seemed to hesitate. It was so slight that he might have been simply searching for the right word to explain easily to the child, but, coming from a man who was so forcefully articulate, it struck an alien note to Briar's ears, and left her wondering,

What did her parchment really say? What did it contain that made Drew reluctant to give her a straight interpretation, as he had done for Tim?

The calligrapher's expression was inscrutable, offering her no clue, and since Drew had spoken to the man in his own language presumably he was not fluent in English, so it was pointless to ask him. The open amusement on Drew's face told her that what the man had written was at his dictation, and he could interpret it easily enough if he chose to. Plainly he did not, unless she asked him first.

Briar's lips tightened. This was simply another way for Drew to force her to do what he wanted, and she refused to give him the satisfaction. She was not a mah-jong tile, to be pushed around at will. Pretending to be content with the oblique answer which he had given to Tim, she slipped the piece of parchment safely into her bag, where it burned its question through the raffia to torment her, until she managed to quieten her curiosity with sudden inspiration. She would ask the Chinese waiter at the hotel. He would be able to tell her.

Her decision enabled her to forget the parchment while they had lunch at a Kashmiri restaurant, which provided a cool retreat from the sticky heat of the streets. It was a hilarious meal, eaten with their fingers off banana-leaf plates, but when the food was first put in front of her Briar viewed the delicious-looking mixture of rice and vegetables with total dismay.

'They've forgotten to bring our knives and forks!' Tim voiced her consternation, and Drew answered,

'They don't use them here. You eat with your fingers—like this, look.'

He scooped up some of his own rice mixture into a neat ball and popped it into his mouth, with a dexterity that told Briar he had done this many times before.

'I haven't brought anything to mop up Tim afterwards,' she protested, and Drew shrugged.

'There's always a place to wash in. Go on, try it,' he urged Tim. 'It will be a new experience for you.'

Nothing loath, the boy followed his uncle's example, and managed to get a commendable amount of food into his mouth after the first one or two tries. Briar's eyes went from her own rice mixture to the two contentedly eating males, and indignation rose in her. It was all right for them— Drew was an adept, expertise made sure he could eat without any danger of a spill, and Tim's age excused him getting himself in a mess. It was different for her. Drew knew it, and patently enjoyed her dilemma.

'Not hungry?' he taunted, his own banana leaf already half empty, and Briar gritted her teeth with frustration. Their energetic morning of sightseeing had left her feeling absolutely hollow. Her one frugal slice of toast at breakfast-time seemed a hundred years away. The spicy aroma rose from her own meal to tantalise her nostrils, and her stomach cried out for the food to be transferred. She gave a hunted look at her spotless cream linen dress, and her stomach—or was it Drew?—won.

Hunger overcame her indignation, and, using a clean and completely inadequate lace-edged handkerchief to augment her napkin, she dipped her fingers into the pile, and ate.

The food provided proved to be as good as it looked, her normally nimble fingers acquired a proficiency she would not have thought possible in so short a time, and soon she was catching up with Drew and Tim.

The meal proceeded merrily. They bet on who could eat with the least spill. Tim gloated, 'You've got rice on your chin, Briar,' and she retaliated swiftly,

'You've got rice on the end of your nose.'

They both turned on Drew whose smug expression said he knew his own face was spotless. 'You've done this before!' they accused him, and his face relaxed in a grin.

'Lots of times. It's the only way to eat this type of meal. I've often been tempted to do it in London, only the possible shock to the waiters stopped me.'

A fleeting thought crossed Briar's mind—nothing would stop this man if he really wanted to do something—but it passed, and her laugh was as carefree as Tim's at the picture he presented, and earned her a keen look from Drew.

'I've never heard you laugh like that before.

She had not laughed like that for a very long time, so long that she scarcely remembered when. But now was not the time to open her heart, and Drew was not the person to reveal its secrets to, and she answered evasively, 'I've never done anything like this before. How do they manage when they have soup?' she giggled, trying to turn the conversation away from herself, but Drew was not to be deterred, and, instead of answering her question, he asked one of his own.

'What *have* you done before? I don't remember seeing you around, either in Warwick or Leamington.'

'I've been living in London for some time,' Briar hedged, resisting his searching look, and when Tim exclaimed,

'Ugh! I'm all sticky!' she grabbed at the opportunity to leave the table.

'Come with me and get a wash, then. We're neither of us fit to be seen.'

The erratic thudding of her pulse was a drumbeat of retreat in her ears, as she hurried Tim towards the washroom. She could feel Drew's reflective gaze on her back, tingling along her spine, and she wondered uncomfortably if her own evasiveness about her private life had merely succeeded in making Drew as curious to know more as his evasiveness about the message on the parchment had made her.

Her mind said there was no reason whatsoever why she should not open up and tell him about her past. Her instinct said there was every reason not to, and, caught between the two, she did not know which to believe. She only knew that she did not want any sympathy from Drew. Her pride shrank from it. He was so strong, so sure of himself, so capable of managing other people's lives as well as his own—the determined way in which he had removed Tim was a clear example—that he would have scant patience with one of life's casualties, and his scorn would be even harder to endure than his sympathy.

In her position, Drew would probably have hurled all the agonising memories into the dustbin of experience, slammed on the lid, and got on with his life without a single backwards glance. Would that she could do the same! But the hurt of the recent past remained with her like a dark bruise, colouring her horizons and sapping her confidence.

None of this showed on Briar's face, however, when she returned with Tim from the washroom. Her expression was outwardly serene and controlled, until Drew shook her composure by remarking, when they got within earshot,

'*Very* nice!'

His teasing look swept over her from tip to toe, and it was that, as much as his actual words, that warmed her cheeks. She could not tell if he was approving her own spotless appearance or the transformation she had wrought in Tim's, and she loathed the flush of too-ready colour to her cheeks, which brought the now familiar spark to Drew's eyes, making her resent the effortless ease with which he was able to bring that colour into play, a process he seemed to enjoy, and used with increasing frequency to torment her.

The colour left her cheeks completely when they took a ride on a cable-car later, travelling from the heights of the main island down to visit an adjoining one. The view from the wide observation windows was magnificent, but Briar's usually good head for heights suddenly deserted her when she noticed the frail-looking thread of wire from which their craft was suspended. To her dismayed gaze, it did not look nearly strong enough to bear the weight of the crowded cable-car.

Tim was quick to spot her discomfiture. He commented, 'I don't think Briar's enjoying this very much, Uncle Drew,' and made her feel even worse.

Drew himself seemed to be quite unaffected. He sat utterly relaxed on the bench seat beside her, and Briar gritted her teeth, fighting for calm when he turned his head and studied her set face.

'I thought you liked flying?'

'I do. This is different. We're only held up on a thread of wire, and it makes me feel like a spider, hanging on to the end of a web.'

'A spider with brown curls would be something new! Never mind, we'll soon be on the other side. Snuggle up to me if it will make you feel any safer.'

Drew did not wait for Briar to accept his invitation. He reached out a long arm and curled it round her waist, drawing her against him, and she wanted to kick herself for letting her nervousness show. What an idiot she was, to give Drew such an opportunity. And how swift he had been to take advantage of it.

Safe was a misnomer. The terrors of the cable-car ride became as nothing compared to the terrors posed by her essentially feminine reaction as Drew pulled her close, and closer. Her pulses began to race as she felt the hardness of his body press against her own, bringing her within range of the faint, expensive aura of the aftershave lotion that he used.

Briar held her breath against it, resisting the subtle invasion of her senses that set her every nerve-end tingling, but Drew's arm held her captive, and for fear she dared not try to struggle free, lest she set the cable-car swinging even more wildly than the stiff breeze swung it now.

At last for very life she had to breathe again, and with each lungful of air she was forced to inhale the subtle, spicy aroma which held an elusive depth that was as difficult to plumb as its wearer.

So close was she that she could feel the strong, steady beat of Drew's heart through the lightweight cotton material of his bush shirt, and it sent messages to her own suddenly unstable organ that made it race almost out of control.

Desperately Briar hoped that Drew would not notice its wild acrobatics, and knew from his derisive downwards glance that she hoped in vain. She closed her eyes against it, using her fear as her excuse, and knew that to be in vain too, since her closed lids failed to shut out the image of a sharply chiselled jawline, and two all-seeing grey eyes, much too close above her own, and seeing—what?

Drew spoke in her ear, and his breath stirred the brown curls nestling against the tiny lobe. 'Don't worry. We'll come back on the ferry.'

Little did he know that she was no longer worried about the return trip. She was far more concerned about what was happening to her on the outward journey, which made neither logic nor sense to her bewildered mind.

It was only after they returned to the hotel that two things struck Briar. Drew had not laughed at her for her craven fear on the cable-car. And, for the first time in months, painful thoughts of Lucy and Philip had not dominated every single waking moment of her day. In working to help Tim forget his problems, she had been able, temporarily, to forget her own.

Her uneasiness returned with renewed force as she acknowledged that it was mainly Drew who was responsible for making her forget.

Tim settled down to write up the details of his eventful day in his diary, but when the boy confessed ruefully, 'I don't know if I can remember all about everything—we did such a lot of things. Will you help me, Uncle Drew?' the latter refused with obvious regret.

'I shan't be able to help you tonight, Tim—I've got to go to another meeting. Ask Briar about the bits you can't remember clearly, and I'll fill in any gaps if you show me what you've written tomorrow morning.'

With an awful conviction Briar knew she would have no difficulty at all in remembering every single detail of their day. It was imprinted on her mind with a vividness that was a warning in itself, but she put it to the back of her mind, and excused the extraordinary clarity of her recollection with the thought, I was just extra noticing, to help Tim with his diary, that's all.

Was it all?

Her pillow seemed to echo the question that night, and could offer no such easy excuse when Drew's face superimposed itself on those of Philip and Lucy in her dreaming mind, and Drew's deep voice followed her as she slipped finally over the edge of sleep, carrying with her his promise, 'I'll see you in the morning.'

The promise was for Tim, of course. But the sleep-eroded barriers of her reason could not help but be glad that it included herself as well.

The next day followed much the same pattern. They flew Tim's kite in the morning, in one of the many beautiful parks that were such a delightful feature of the city. Local families were out in force with their own children, and it took an effort of will on Briar's part to resist the temptation to pretend that they were a family too, like all the others. But that path led to danger, and sternly Briar redirected her feet on to safer ground, that of an employee, engaged to look after another woman's child.

It did not detract from her enjoyment, however, when Drew hired a boat and took them out to see the *kelongs*, the wooden shacks on stilts from which the local fishermen operated, even though, when they got there, she and Drew clashed once again over the controversial subject of a woman's role.

This time it was merely light-hearted fencing. It did not have the sharpness of their previous exchange on the plane, but it served to reinforce

Drew's uncompromising stance when Tim begged, 'Can we go on one, and have a look?'

'You and I can go,' said Drew, and, although he spoke to Tim, his amused look was directed at Briar. 'Briar will have to stay on the boat. The fishermen don't allow women on the *kelongs*.'

'How typical!' Briar exploded. 'Male chauvinists evidently aren't confined to our own country. The fishermen there won't allow woman on their boats either.'

'Why not?' Tim asked innocently, and Drew replied drily,

'Women are bad luck.'

Not *supposed to be* bad luck. *Are* bad luck. His direct phrasing was a sweeping condemnation, and it goaded Briar to retaliate. Indignant words trembled on the tip of her tongue, and just in time she remembered that Tim was awake this time, and listening, ready to drink in everything that she said.

A row between herself and Drew might easily undermine the child's confidence, just as he was beginning to settle down. It might even, dreadful thought, bring him to share his uncle's outrageous viewpoint. Quickly Briar reined back her stinging retort and let her eyes speak for her instead, as she directed a vitriolic look at Drew.

The swift uptilting of his well-cut lips registered their message, and jeered at her frustration, and he left Briar to glower helplessly from the boat rail as he handed Tim up to a smiling fisherman, then followed himself, leaving her to wonder what had happened in his life to turn him off women.

She shrugged. Philip had happened, to turn her off men, so that made them even.

At the end of their day out Tim was tired but happy, and he laughed gaily as they swung him between them up the hotel steps and in through the wide entrance doors.

When they got inside, Elizabeth was waiting for them in the foyer.

CHAPTER FOUR

BRIAR knew that it was Elizabeth even before Tim dragged his hands free and bounded across the foyer shouting, 'Mummy! Mummy!'

At the sound of his cry, the woman rose swiftly from her chair, tossing aside the magazine she had been leafing through. Tim raced into her wide-stretched arms, and they closed about him, clasping him hungrily to her.

Over the child's head Elizabeth's gaze embraced Drew and Briar, and there was no love in it for either of them. The grey glance, so like Drew's, carried an unforgiving anger that bid fair to reduce them both to ashes on the spot.

'How *could* you do this to me?' she ground out, and her eyes flicked from her brother to rest contemptuously on Briar. 'You and that—that— *woman*!'

'Careful, Elizabeth.' Drew's low tone matched his surname.

'Careful?' The laugh that accompanied it held a note of hysteria. 'I've stopped being careful—or hadn't you noticed? Perhaps you've been too busy, like Robert.'

'You know I've tried to get Robert to delegate, to allow himself more time off.'

'Delegate!' Elizabeth's scorn ground the word into dust. 'Robert's indispensable—at least, he is

68

to his work. Tim and I have to get along without him as best we can.'

'Mummy?'

The plea was frightened, choked with impending tears. Tim's face held a pinched look, so different from the laughing, carefree child who had swung between them up the hotel steps. A furious anger stirred inside Briar at the change. How *could* they? Whatever Elizabeth and Robert were doing to each other, how could they do this to Tim?

Drew said, 'Take Tim upstairs, Briar, and get him washed ready for supper.'

'Tim's not going anywhere with that woman. In fact, he's not going out of my sight ever again.'

'Then let's all go upstairs, where we can discuss this sensibly, and in private.'

An influx of chattering guests flooding into the foyer from a tourist coach reinforced Drew's command, and Elizabeth turned, tight-lipped, and followed him, but on the way she kept one arm protectively around Tim, and stationed the boy as far from Briar as possible in the lift.

As she watched her, a cold feeling clutched at Briar's stomach. Her fears about Elizabeth's re-action to Drew's taking off with Tim were well founded. It was clear that the boy's mother blamed her, Briar, as much as Drew, perhaps more, and the other woman's promise confirmed her unease the moment they reached the privacy of the suite.

'You haven't heard the last of this from me,' Elizabeth warned Briar, and Drew intervened sharply,

'Cease fire, will you, until after dinner?'

His words said, 'Cease fire'. His look commanded, Not in front of Tim. The glance he shot at his sister held all the ice of an Arctic blizzard, and it penetrated Elizabeth's anger, stemming her flow of furious words.

Briar cut into the brief silence. 'I'll go and make a cup of tea.' She hurried into the tiny kitchenette, and shut the door behind her, but her respite was short-lived. Hardly a minute had gone by before the door opened again, to admit Tim.

'Uncle Drew said you wanted me to help you carry things.'

Briar schooled her expression to calm. 'The kettle hasn't boiled yet. We'll have to wait for a minute or two.'

She toed the door closed behind Tim. The brief time alone would enable Drew and his sister space for a short skirmish, if that was what they wanted, out of the boy's hearing. Her own position was a delicate one, but she intended to do her utmost to make sure they did not use the child as ammunition in their fight. She was being unfair to Drew in this, and she knew it, but one glance at the boy's woebegone expression hardened her heart. Tim faltered, 'Mummy's angry.'

Briar affected unconcern. 'She isn't angry with you, poppet. It's just jet lag, I expect—it affects grown-ups too, you know. Don't you remember how cross you felt the day after we landed? You didn't cheer up until we got your teddy.'

Tim was cuddling the toy to him now, and Briar's anger increased. The child had forgotten his need for the teddy during the last two fascinating days of going out and about. He had only remembered it at bedtime. Now he clutched it to him as if he intended never to be parted from it again, and Briar vowed silently to herself, Elizabeth hasn't heard the last of this from me either. Out loud she remarked, on a sudden inspiration, 'I expect your mummy's disappointed too. She probably didn't get the part in the play when she went for her audition, and you know how badly you feel when you've had a big disappointment.'

If she read the signs aright, Tim should be a past master in handling disappointment. He had had plenty of practice in coping with broken promises in his young life.

'Do you think so? She didn't say anything about the audition.' Doubt and dawning hope flitted like April shadows across the small face upturned to her own.

Briar said practically, as she turned to attend to the now boiling kettle, 'If your mummy had been given the part, she'd still be at the theatre, busy rehearsing it, wouldn't she? But she's come here instead, to spend the rest of the holiday with you. So be extra nice to her. Show her the diary you're writing for her. She's bound to be pleased that you've gone to so much trouble for her. It'll make up for not having been given the part in the play.'

Fervently Briar hoped she was not mistaken, as she dispensed the tea a few minutes later in an atmosphere that was as dark as the liquid itself, then sat through the evening meal afterwards, doing her best to remain at least outwardly unaffected by the strain which fairly crackled around the table, like a time-bomb ticking away just underneath the surface, and due to explode the very moment Tim was fast asleep.

The child himself came near to igniting the fuse once or twice. After supper he settled down at the table as usual, to write his diary, and when Elizabeth took her chair to join him, and offered, 'Let me help you,' Tim answered with the unwitting cruelty of childhood,

'I'll give it to you to read afterwards. Briar has to help me to write it, because she was there and you weren't.'

Elizabeth flinched, but she read through what Tim had written afterwards, what there was of it until now. She remarked, 'Your new swimming-trunks sound nice. You must show them to me in the morning.'

'They're lovely. Uncle Drew bought us both a swimsuit—Briar and me. Mine is red, with a white stripe down the side.'

'So Drew bought you a swimsuit as well? I expect you chose one of the designer quality?' Elizabeth enquired with barbed sweetness, and added, *sotto voce*, 'And what else, I wonder?'

In front of Tim, Briar dared not voice the angry words that longed to tumble from the tip of her tongue, and she turned away, fighting for control, but when bedtime came, Tim insisted that she go with him as usual, to kiss him and his teddy goodnight.

'She always does,' he explained to his mother, innocently unaware of the effect his words were having on the two women, whose eyes met above the narrow bed with its bright counterpane, Elizabeth's eyes hurting, hating, accusing Briar of deliberately usurping her own position, and promising a reckoning later on.

She fired the first salvo when they returned to the sitting-room together, although, mindful of the fact that Tim was probably still drowsily awake, she was careful to keep her voice low.

She turned on Briar the moment the boy's bedroom door was closed behind them, and promised in a voice that vibrated with anger, 'The moment I get back to England I'll prosecute you for taking Tim away from me. The law takes a harsh view of women who steal children!'

'Go ahead,' Drew drawled from the depths of his armchair, and Briar stared.

'Just a minute!' she exploded indignantly, and had the feeling that she had said much the same thing to Drew before, with the same non-effect. He continued calmly, as if she had not spoken,

'If you prosecute Briar, I'll bring a counter-prosecution against you. The law takes an equally harsh view of mothers who abandon their children.'

Elizabeth swung on him, aghast. 'I didn't abandon Tim! I left him with you.'

'You knew I had to go abroad that week. I warned you that I had to attend business meetings out here.'

'Meetings, meetings!' Elizabeth's laugh was mirthless. 'I'm sick and tired of hearing about business meetings! They're just an excuse to get out of doing something you don't want to do anyway. I simply don't listen any more.'

'If you had listened, you might have realised the difficulty you were putting me in when you took off to go to that audition.'

'For all the good I did there, I might as well not have gone!'

Briar thought, I'm glad I was right about that, for Tim's sake, but, before the relief had time to register, Elizabeth swept on with a contemptuous toss of her head in Drew's direction,

'You can't complain, Drew. My not being there gave you just the excuse you wanted to come away with *her*.'

Drew straightened in his chair, and his expression was like granite.

'One more suggestion like that, and——'

'And what, Drew?' Elizabeth faced her brother, her body rigid with tension. 'You may be Robert's boss, but you're not mine. I don't have to do as I'm told. And, whether you like it or not, you're going to have to listen to a lot more suggestions of the same kind when I take you and your girlfriend to court.'

'I'll leave you to discuss this on your own.' Briar turned away, sickened, and Drew snapped her to a halt with,

'Stay where you are! This concerns you just as much as it does me.' He turned back to his sister and addressed her harshly. 'If you take legal action, you wouldn't have a leg to stand on. But if you insist on trying, you'll leave me no alternative but to apply for custody of Tim, on the grounds that neither you nor Robert appear capable of giving the boy a settled background.'

Elizabeth's mouth dropped open, and her face went chalk-white. She seemed to have difficulty in forcing her words out, and, when they came, they were a disbelieving croak. 'You wouldn't dare to do such a thing to me, your own sister?'

'If you force me to, I will. You're an adult, and capable of fending for yourself. Tim's a child, and he can't, and I refuse to stand by and see the boy torn in two by parents who seem incapable of sorting out their affairs sensibly.'

Drew waited for his bombshell to take effect, then went on more quietly, 'I suggest we call it a day. A night's rest might bring you to your senses. If there's anything more to be said on the subject, we can talk it out in the morning.' He cut across his sister's attempt to argue with a brusque, 'Which room are you booked into?'

'I didn't reserve a room. I was too worried to think about anything except——'

'In that case, I'll go and see about getting one for you.'

'You needn't bother,' snapped Elizabeth. 'If you think I'm leaving Tim, you're mistaken. I'll sleep on the floor of his room, if necessary, rather than leave him with *her* for a moment longer. I won't be parted from him again, Drew, I don't care what you say!' Elizabeth's voice rose dangerously, close to hysteria. 'The moment my back's turned, she might take it into her head to make off with him again somewhere else.'

'You're talking nonsense!'

'Leave it, Drew,' Briar intervened. Elizabeth was hurt and angry, and lashing out to ease her own pain. Too well, Briar knew the agony of being parted from a child.

Surprised by her own self-control, she offered as calmly as she could manage, 'There's no need for

Elizabeth to be parted from Tim. She can have my room.' She turned to the distraught woman. 'It adjoins Tim's room, so you'll hear if he stirs in the night. I'll move out. There's bound to be a room vacant in a hotel of this size.'

'There's no need for that,' said Drew. 'If Elizabeth has your room, you can have mine, and I'll move out of the suite and get another one for myself.'

'You should feel quite at home in Drew's room,' Elizabeth said waspishly as the door closed behind her brother, and Briar took in a hissing breath.

'That was totally uncalled-for,' she began hotly. 'I——'

'Mummy?'

A small pyjamaed figure stumbled sleepily into view, clutching his teddy bear, and both women spun round.

'I'm here, darling.' In a trice, Elizabeth was on her knees beside her son, and Briar checked her instinctive step towards him. Tim was no longer in her charge. She stood to one side as he mumbled,

'I'm glad you're real. I thought you were only a dream. I was afraid when I woke up you'd be gone away again.'

'Of course I'm real. And I shan't go away ever again. I'm going to sleep in the room next to yours.'

'That's Briar's room.'

'It's mine now.' The look Elizabeth threw at Briar held triumph. 'Come back to bed now, Tim, and I'll tuck you up and read you a story until you go to sleep.'

The door closed behind mother and son, shutting Briar out, and she slowly set about removing her

belongings from her room. As she picked up her
toilet articles one by one, she tried to scold away
the depression that enveloped her by telling herself
that it had to happen some time, and she should
be glad for Tim.

She *was* glad for Tim, but the chasm of emptiness left in her heart when she'd lost Lucy looked
even emptier without the child to fill the gap, and
her eyes blurred with tears as she gazed down into
the dark depths which seemed so much darker by
contrast with the stolen happiness of the last days.

The floor staff created a welcome diversion by
arriving to change the beds, then Drew returned to
announce,

'I've been able to reserve a room just along the
corridor from here—number ten. Give me a ring
on the intercom, if you have any problems during
the night.'

'What problems can there be? Tim's happy now
that his mother's here. I'll see about getting a flight
back home in the morning.'

'I engaged you for the whole month.' Drew's
voice was uncompromising.

'I'm not needed now,' Briar protested, and the
knowledge brought with it an unexpected wave of
desolation that made her bite her lip to suppress its
tremble, as she faced Drew, a small, valiant figure
with desolation dulling her eyes, while her chin rose
in the determined tilt her solicitor had learned to
know and admire.

Drew studied her for what seemed an endless
minute before he answered, 'I shall hold you to your
contract, just the same. For all I know, Elizabeth
might take it into her head to disappear again, and

then what would happen to Tim while I was out at meetings?'

Briar could give him no answer. There was none to give, and, if there had been, she felt incapable of doing so. Relief at being able to stay met the desolation head-on, the one just as irrational as the other, and, bewildered by both, she choked on words, and had to rely on a silent nod.

It seemed to satisfy Drew, however. He said, 'I'll take the things I need just for tonight, and remove the rest from my room tomorrow morning.'

Briar was still standing where he left her when he returned with a small overnight case in one hand and a dressing-gown slung over his arm. A dropping tiredness descended on her, leaving her feeling drained, a tiredness that owed nothing to the hectic, happy day of sightseeing that lay behind them.

Drew paused on his way to the door, his eyes all-seeing on her face. 'Go to bed,' he commanded. 'You look all in.'

'I will ... I am ...'

She was stammering, unable to meet his look, wishing he would go away, and wishing he would stay. Her mind refused to think clearly, and she blamed it on the tiredness, until Drew made the turmoil worse, and gave the lie to her excuse.

He slid the case to the floor and piled his dressing-gown on top of it, then, reaching out his hand, he cupped her chin in strong fingers and tilted her face up to meet his penetrating gaze.

'Are my family giving you a hard time, Briar rose?' he murmured.

The sudden uncharacteristic change from brisk authority to gentleness was Briar's undoing. It penetrated her carefully erected defences, and made her weak to resist him when he lowered his head, turning his hair into a dark crescent above her as his lips searched her own for the answer.

Shock waves of sensation washed over her at his touch. They flung aside the tiredness and set every nerve tingling, and despairingly Briar knew that her armour was not proof against this man's charisma. Would any woman's be? Feelings that she had thought were long since dead, killed by Philip's behaviour, sprang into urgent life—painful, agonising life.

The pain seared her. The instinctive response of her lips against his frightened her. Her arms raised of their own accord, trying to link themselves round his neck, but forcefully she willed them to push against him instead, using her small, balled fists to beat his chest, until at last he lifted his head and looked down at her quizzically.

Briar sucked in a shuddering breath. Drew's eyes were dark pools above her, grey as mountain tarns inviting her to swim in their mysterious depths. With an effort that almost cost her the last of her reeling senses, she dragged herself back from the brink.

'Let me go!' she choked, and, wrenching herself free from his slackened hold, she fled into the room he had just vacated, and slammed the door shut behind her. Her trembling legs refused to carry her any further, and she leaned back against the supporting wood, waiting for her heart to calm its violent hammering, another pain almost as bad as the first.

If Drew chose to follow her through the door, she would not have the strength to hold it against him, and he might draw her, against her will, down into the depths of those grey pools, to drown.

She shivered as if with an ague, and a question tracked uninvited across her mind. Which door did she mean? She shook her head, trying to shake her muddled thoughts into some kind of order. She meant the door of the room, of course. The door to her heart had been locked and bolted long ago, and she had thrown away the key. But the question remained to torment her long after she heard the outer door to the suite open, then quietly close on Drew's firm step, and only then did the wild fluttering of her heart begin to resume its normal beat.

In spite of her weariness, sleep eluded Briar. Drew had left the suite, but part of him still remained in the room with her, like a ghostly presence. She tried to shut her tired mind against it, but she could not close her nostrils to the faint, pervasive smell of his aftershave lotion, which lingered on the air to remind her that this was the bed he had slept in last night, the pillow his head had rested upon, and which now refused to give rest to her own.

She slept late the next morning, and breakfasted alone. Dark rings circled her eyes, mute evidence of her sleepless night, and the silence of the suite oppressed her.

Elizabeth and Tim were not in evidence. A cautious peep into Tim's bedroom revealed his suitcase and clothes still intact, so they had not left. What had taken them out so early? Had the boy's mother ignored Drew's warning, and gone to visit a lawyer after all? Had she decided to take action right away, and not leave matters until she returned to England?

Briar's fickle appetite vanished altogether, and she slid her unwanted slice of toast into the waste-bin. Should she call Drew on the intercom and find out? Her hand was already reaching out for the house telephone when her wristwatch told her that he would most probably be at a meeting by now, and not still in his room.

He had not mentioned an early appointment last night, but the events of the fraught evening made it understandable that he might forget. Briar was halfway though her cup of coffee when the door burst open, and Tim ran into the room, closely followed by Elizabeth and Drew. The boy was carrying his kite.

'We've been flying it in the park, Briar,' he cried. 'You should have come with us, it was lovely!'

'You were tired, so I wouldn't let him disturb you,' Drew excused her exclusion from the outing, and Briar thought bleakly that Drew had already disturbed her a lot more than merely getting up early to fly a kite would have done. But the boy's uncle was not to know that, and, averting her face from his keen gaze, she turned away to take her cup and saucer back to the kitchenette, aware of Drew explaining behind her,

'I'll be out all day, but I should be back in time for dinner. Look after your mother and Briar for me until then, Tim.'

Elizabeth remained silent, her expression brooding, and Briar's heart misgave her at the prospect of spending a whole day in the other woman's hostile company. Without Drew to support her, she did not feel equal to a confrontation.

She replied automatically to Drew's parting, 'See you,' and answered Tim's plea, 'Shall we swim when your breakfast's gone down, Briar?' with an evasive,

'Perhaps, later on. I want to go shopping first.'

Now was her opportunity to browse through the shops that had held so much attraction before, so why did they seem to be so unattractive now? Briar's mind wrestled with the question, and Elizabeth had to repeat herself before the sense of what the other woman said impinged upon her consciousness.

'Don't go, Briar. Or, if you do, let Tim and me come along with you. I—I'd like to talk to you.'

Briar regarded her warily. 'If it's about what you were saying to me last night, then talk it over with Drew.' Her voice was hard. 'It's his responsibility, not mine. Whatever you might think, I'm only a hired hand.'

'I don't think anything.' Elizabeth had the grace to look ashamed. 'Drew took us into the park this morning, and while Tim was flying his kite he explained everything to me.'

Elizabeth's obvious sincerity disarmed Briar, and when later she sat beside Elizabeth at the poolside, watching Tim splashing happily in the water with the small son of another hotel guest, the boy's mother apologised,

'I said some unforgivable things to you last night.'

The older woman's face looked ravaged, and Briar thought with quick compassion, She didn't sleep any better than I did. Aloud she answered gently, 'You were tired and upset last night. Why not just forget it and start again, from this morning?'

The quick brightening of Elizabeth's troubled expression rewarded her generosity. 'Would you? I feel we could be friends. Drew told me you were staying on.'

Briar answered carefully, 'There isn't any need for me to stay on, now you're here.'

Elizabeth reached across and placed an impulsive hand on her arm. 'I wish you would stay—honestly, Briar. I'd be so grateful for your company. I need someone I can talk to—beside Drew, I mean. Men don't understand.'

They spent the afternoon browsing round the shops, enjoying their foray together as only women could, and when Drew returned they were happily discussing some bargains over a cup of tea, while Tim sprawled between them, contentedly engrossed in a new comic paper.

'Peace has broken out,' Drew deduced, and Elizabeth smiled.

'We've spent a lovely day together. I'm glad Briar's going to stay on.'

'It's just as well you are,' her brother replied drily, 'because we decided at the meeting today to hold an early site inspection. It means I have to fly out into the interior tomorrow morning, so you'll have to keep one another company for a week or two.'

'Can we come with you, Uncle Drew?' Mention of the interior made Tim forget the fictional adventures of his comic hero for the real one being enacted on his doorstep, and his face reflected his disappointment when Drew shook his head.

'You can't come with me into the rain forests. The jungle's no place for women and children. Malaria's rife in the interior, and you've got no protection against it.'

'You're going there,' the little boy objected.

'I've been taking the necessary precautions, so I'm reasonably safe.' Drew turned to Briar. 'I'll remove my things from your room before I go, then I must contact base, to arrange about the flight.'

'Will you be going on Concorde?' Tim forgot his disappointment, and Drew laughed.

'The landing strip we're building isn't long enough to take a normal jet, let alone Concorde. I shall be going by helicopter.'

He went away, and when Briar entered her room later to dress for the evening meal all trace of his belongings was gone, as was the smell of his after-shave lotion, which the efficient air-conditioning had removed during the day. The room was once more just an impersonal hotel stop-over, and, no matter that she derided her own reaction, Briar shrank from its cold unwelcome.

Quickly she slipped her dress over her head and tightened the belt about her slim waist. She turned to the dressing-table to pick up the lace-edged handkerchief which matched the delicate embroidery of wild roses round the hem of her skirt, and frowned down at the blank space of polished wood where she had placed it.

The handkerchief was not there. A brief hunt across the floor met with no success, and she shrugged, and reached into her drawer for another. The handkerchief's only use was as an ornament, to tuck into her bracelet to allow the single embroidered rose to show. Perhaps the room staff had mistaken it for laundry and removed it for washing. If so, it would come back to her the next day.

Dinner that night was a relaxed meal, in total contrast to that of the evening before, and when a car called for Drew early the next morning Briar stood with Elizabeth and Tim on the hotel steps to wave him goodbye.

'Take the ladies out and show them Singapore, just as I showed it to you,' was his parting instruction to Tim, then he was ducking into the car beside the chauffeur, with no more than a casual wave of his hand in farewell.

Bleakness descended on Briar as she watched the limousine speed away. Had Drew deliberately chosen to take leave of them in the foyer, knowing that public expressions of affection were frowned on in this land of formal courtesies? Was he regretting his kiss, and taking this way out rather than repeat it?

Reason told Briar that Drew's kisses were no more than mere opportunism, and held no meaning, but in spite of herself her lips bemoaned their lack, and the emptiness remained with her as she accompanied Elizabeth and Tim on their sightseeing trip through the city, and, although she tried to lose herself in the pleasure of exploration, the shine was gone, along with Drew.

Tim thrived on his new role as escort. He insisted on them repeating the trishaw ride, for his mother's benefit, and when they descended from the vehicle Briar knew it was irrational of her to mourn the lack of arms to lift her down, since she had shrunk away from them before, but she could not help it.

The pavements seemed hotter and more exhausting than before, and she found it difficult to concentrate on the multitude of interests surrounding her. Her mind persisted in following Drew, and her ears strained for the rattle of helicopter rotors above the noise and bustle of the city, and that was silly too, since Drew had refused Tim's plea to be able to see the aircraft because the flying field was a long car ride out of town.

They lunched off conventional plates, using knives and forks, and the food did not seem to be half so appetising as that which they had eaten with Drew, from off banana leaves, and using only their fingers, and Briar's energy began to flag long before they returned to the hotel.

Drew had been gone for nearly a week when Robert arrived.

It was like a re-run of the same scenario, only with a change of cast, and it was Elizabeth who was in control this time, both of herself and of the situation.

Briar noticed that Robert did not receive the same ecstatic welcome from his son that Tim had given to his mother, and when she tactfully suggested they go for a swim together, and leave his parents on their own, the boy made no objection.

Robert's increased pallor registered Tim's indifference, and, although she privately considered that it was no more than the man deserved, Briar could not help but feel sorry for him.

An hour later she was beginning to wonder for how much longer she should allow Tim to splash in the water when Elizabeth and Robert came to join them. Robert was dressed in swimming-trunks, and, responding to the mute appeal in his eyes, she tossed the play ball to him and swung herself out of the water, leaving him a clear field with his son.

Elizabeth's eyes were determined, as Briar dropped on to a chair beside her and reached for a towel. She gave her hair a vigorous rub, wondering what to say, when Elizabeth broke what threatened to become an awkward silence between them.

'Shock tactics seem to work,' she said slowly.

Briar sent her a quick upward glance, and a slight smile touched the other woman's lips. 'Robert panicked even more badly than I did when he got home and found Tim and me missing.'

Briar stared. Elizabeth had used exactly the same tactics on her husband that Drew had used on her. Elizabeth was more like her brother than she had been led to believe. Out loud she asked, 'Will it last, do you think?'

She felt justified in asking, since Elizabeth had taken her completely into her confidence on that first day they spent together, and the older woman replied with equal frankness,

'Maybe not for ever. He might need a reminder now and then. Robert's wrapped up in his work, and it means so much to him that I wouldn't try to part him from it.'

The quietly spoken words were a measure of the depths of Elizabeth's love for her husband, which could look facts in the face and still remain intact, even while she took stern measures to deal with him. Briar's respect for her increased, as she went on,

'Just the same, Robert knows now that he's got to make room in his life for Tim and me, or risk losing us altogether. That was why I went to that audition. I didn't want the wretched part, but I had to jolt Robert to his senses somehow. Coming out to Singapore's been even more effective. Robert's aware that he's nearly lost Tim already, and he'll have to work hard to get him back.'

Briar nodded without speaking. The boy's casual, 'Oh, hello, Daddy,' and his immediate return to the book he had been reading when Robert walked in was something that would stay with her for a long time. She hoped, for all their sakes, that it would stay with Robert too, and offered,

'I'll move out of the suite and leave you to yourselves.'

She was taken aback by Elizabeth's firm refusal. 'No, you must stay in your room. Robert can have Drew's room for now. Number ten, isn't it?'

'Yes, but——'

Elizabeth cut across her protest. 'Robert's got to earn the right to be with Tim and me again. I won't allow him to persuade me, as he has done before. It will be too easy if he shares the suite.'

She did not say, if he shares my bed, but the implication was strong, and there was a small silence before she went on ruefully, 'It's been partly my fault—I've been too accepting, too ready to let Robert put his work first. But this time I won't weaken. I daren't, for all our sakes. Instead of me always being left behind to cope alone, from now on Robert and I will work things out together.'

'I hope it comes out right for you.'

The wretchedness of it not coming out right for herself added conviction to her words, and drew a questioning look from Elizabeth, who answered with a confidence Briar envied.

'It will. It may take a little time, but it will be worth it in the long run.'

The next morning Briar was surprised to see suitcases lined up at the suite door.

'We're going on holiday!' Tim announced excitedly. 'Daddy's got a whole month away from work—at least, he has for now.' The qualification dimmed Robert's smile, and it faded still further when the little boy added wistfully, 'I wish you were coming with us as well, Briar.'

Because the boy knew she would keep her promise and stay with him. Briar said gently, 'Your mummy and daddy will be there. I have to stay here, to wait for your Uncle Drew.'

'I'll take my teddy along too,' Tim decided cautiously, and Briar heard the faint hiss of Robert's indrawn breath as the innocent arrow struck home.

The boy's father was going to have to work very hard indeed before he regained his son's trust. With well-timed diplomacy, Elizabeth laid the first foundation stone for him.

'Robert's always promised to take us to visit Thailand when he had the opportunity. Isn't it lovely that he remembered, now he's got some holiday from the laboratory at last?'

Briar marvelled silently—he doesn't deserve her! What man did deserve the sacrifices a woman was prepared to make for love? she asked herself cynically, and was confounded by the look Robert threw at his wife, a mixture of surprise, and gratitude, and reawakened love that promised better things.

Good luck to them, Briar wished as she waved the small family on their way an hour later, then returned slowly upstairs to the now depopulated suite.

How quiet it was! She turned to the table to pick up the letter Elizabeth had left for her to give to Drew on his return. She had told Briar briefly what it contained. Words of explanation for their sudden departure. Words of thanks, for her brother's part in bringing herself and Robert together again.

Briar went into her room and opened her shoulder-bag to slip the note safely inside. She did not want a member of the kindly and ever-helpful hotel staff to mistake it for general mail and pop it into the posting-box for her.

The capacious carrying capacity of the bag still held the bargains she had bought on the second quick shopping trip with Elizabeth the evening before, to equip Robert suitably for his unexpected holiday. During the foray, Briar had been tempted to buy some pretty panties and lacy bras to match, and a mix-'n-match set of cotton trousers and tops which she was unable to resist. She must remember to take them out of her bag later, and put them in her dressing-table drawer.

She lodged the envelope in the side pocket of the bag, next to the small square parchment bearing the mysterious Chinese script. 'A kind of— promise,' Drew had described it.

Now was her opportunity to discover exactly what it meant, before Drew returned. She took it out, ready to show the Chinese waiter when he brought the trolley with her evening meal, but when he arrived through the door with his customary smiling, 'Good evening,' her courage failed her.

Memory of the mischievous laughter that lit Drew's eyes, and dared her to ask for a translation, rose to taunt her, daring her to ask for one now. 'A kind of—promise.' A promise of what? Suddenly confused, she rescued the piece of parchment from off the table where she had left it in readiness, and hid it instead, while the waiter laid out the dishes.

It was cowardice. But what if the translation was something that would cause her embarrassment on hearing it from a stranger? Was that the reason for Drew's inner laughter, and his silent challenge?

Briar's courage was not equal to the test. Deriding herself, she yet waited until the man had left the room before she returned the parchment shamefacedly to its original resting place, next to Elizabeth's letter.

She frowned as she contemplated the letter. For how long would Drew be gone? A week or two could mean any length of time, long or short. Which meant that Elizabeth and Robert might well be back before Drew. Her frown deepened as she remembered Elizabeth's urgent,

'It's very important to me that Drew gets my letter as soon as possible. I want him to know that everything's working out well for us, mainly thanks to him.'

What would Elizabeth think if she returned and found the letter still undelivered? If it could be posted, there would be no problem. But until the island runway was completed, and the new air service began, Briar doubted if the jungle-clad interior which had temporarily swallowed Drew would boast such a thing as a postal service.

There *was* one other way.

Hardly daring to contemplate the plan which arrived unbidden in her mind, Briar hurried across the room and bent over the telephone pad on the desk. There it was, in Drew's bold and unmistakable hand, the telephone number he used to contact 'base', wherever that might be, and arrange for his helicopter flight into the interior.

Not giving herself time in which to think, Briar pressed the dialling buttons quickly, then held her breath, hoping fervently that the person on the other end of the line might understand English. Her own linguistic accomplishments did not encompass the language which she had heard Drew use frequently since their arrival.

'Hello?' The voice on the other end of the line was only faintly accented, and Briar went weak with relief.

'I've got an important letter for Mr Steel.' Hurriedly she blurted out her message, one half of her mind fluent in its invention, while the other half looked on, aghast at her temerity. 'I need to hand it to him myself. I'm his personal assistant, I flew out from England with him.'

How easily the words flowed from her tongue! The truth, but not the whole truth, and designed to mislead. Briar's conscience winced, while an imp inside her urged her to take no heed. If her listener chose to misinterpret what she said, it was not her fault, was it?

Her listener offered laconically, 'I'm taking the kite that way in the morning, with some supplies for one of the other islands. If you really must deliver the letter yourself, I can drop you off on the way. I'll send a car for you first thing.'

It was done. There was no backing out now. Briar found she was trembling as she put down the receiver. How easy it had been! Too easy. Impulsively she had committed herself to chasing after Drew, with no thought for what his reaction might be when she arrived, unheralded, on site.

CHAPTER FIVE

THE flight took much longer than Briar expected.

The helicopter droned on for what seemed like hours, and, forced into inactivity, she had leisure in which to question the wisdom of her journey. Drew's adamant, 'The jungle's no place for women and children,' rang in her ears like a knell.

It was too late to do anything about it now, but as the time ticked by she grew more and more apprehensive, until at last she could sit in silence no longer.

'How much further?' she asked her companion. She had to raise her voice above the clatter of the rotor-blades, and the young Indian pilot called back,

'Still quite a way to go yet.'

'I thought helicopters were only used for short journeys?'

'These are long-haul machines, the kind they use on the oil rigs. In fact, this 'copter belongs to the oil company. It's on loan until the string of landing strips is completed right across the islands, and we can decide on the best aircraft to use for our purpose.'

He turned his attention back to his instruments and left Briar once more to her uneasy thoughts. A seemingly endless expanse of glittering ocean passed below them, and as the miles added up her tension increased, and suddenly crystallised on a row of dark dots that appeared in the water ahead of them, like a string of unevenly spaced beads. Her stomach told her that the helicopter was beginning to lose height towards them.

They got closer, and the dots turned a dark green, and Briar realised she was looking down on the upper canopy of thick jungle. Her heart began to race.

At any moment now she would be seeing Drew again. Perhaps he was already there, looking up at the machine and wondering what was the purpose of its unscheduled visit.

What sort of welcome would she receive when she stepped down from the helicopter? Within the space of the next few minutes she was due to find out.

She peered anxiously downwards. The pilot was making for the largest of the islands in the string. A gap became evident in what had looked, from a distance, to be dense, unbroken green. The helicopter hovered over it, and Briar could make out ant-like figures on the ground below them. She strained her eyes, attempting to identify Drew among them, but they were too far away as yet for this to be possible.

At the sight of the aircraft the figures scattered to one side of the small, open space, and stood looking up, except for one who remained in the centre of the clearing, and began to semaphore with his arms, guiding the pilot down.

Immediately the helicopter began to descend, and Briar's mouth went dry. In minutes—seconds—she would come face to face with Drew, and he would greet her—how? Would he be furious with her for coming on such a trivial excuse as having to deliver a letter?

What if he was? He can't eat you, she told herself robustly. It was not as if her visit was likely to interrupt his work for any length of time. She would explain about Elizabeth and Robert, much more clearly than the letter could, and deliver her missive, the pilot would pick her up on his return trip, and that would be that.

That would be final. It hit her, forcefully, that she would not be seeing Drew again after today. By intruding on his island in the interior she had made herself redundant earlier than she would otherwise have been, since he could not argue against her going, now that Robert and Elizabeth had taken their son back into their own charge and gone away with him.

There was absolutely no reason now for her to remain, and the remembered bleakness that the knowledge had brought with it before returned with renewed force, so that it was an effort to pull herself together and try to appear outwardly unconcerned when the pilot helped her out of the aircraft and on to the dusty ground outside.

'Visitor for you!' he called out to the man who had signalled him down, and to Briar he said, 'See you on my way back.' With that, he started up the rotor-blades again, denying further speech, and Briar raised her hand in a wave and tried in vain to quell the fluttering nerves of her stomach as she turned to greet the signaller.

It was not Drew. Reaction set in, and sick disappointment washed over her.

Where was Drew? Briar looked round, but there was no sign of the familiar tall, broad-shouldered figure among the gang of men who now began to resume the tasks they had been engaged on when the helicopter arrived.

She felt nonplussed. Drew's possible absence from the site was something that had not occurred to her. Surely, in such an isolated spot, it was not unreasonable to expect him to appear to greet the helicopter pilot, and discover the reason for his unscheduled visit?

Her eyes widened on the man who came towards her. He was of medium height, black-haired, and his skin, or as much of it as was visible, was a pale brown. The rest was almost completely covered by tattoos. Complicated leaf and scroll patterns covered his face from forehead to chin, and most of the upper parts of his torso. Briar swallowed hard.

She must have been mad, to come all this way just to deliver a letter to Drew! It could easily have waited until he returned. What on earth had possessed her, to do such a crazy thing? For all she knew, Drew might be away on one of the other islands, or even, by now, on his way back to Singapore by another aircraft, and in his absence, how was she to explain her unexpected appearance to this colourfully decorated stranger? Sign language would surely be inadequate for such a task.

The man stopped a pace distant from her and remarked pleasantly, 'Have you come to see Drew?'

Her relief was so great that, in spite of his bizarre appearance, Briar felt she could have hugged him. Of course! The pilot had spoken to him in English.

In this country of many languages, it was used as a common currency by all. She must be losing her grip to have overlooked the obvious. She managed a commendably cool, 'I have, but he doesn't seem to be around,' and left the explanation of his absence to the stranger.

He obliged with, 'He's up-river,' and sent her spirits plummeting, then added, 'He went at first light, so he should be back any time now,' and set them soaring again.

Their gymnastics left her feeling slightly dizzy, and to block out the possible explanation she answered primly, 'I'll wait,' and felt an urge to giggle.

Her reply sounded like that of a mid-Victorian miss presenting her calling card. The incongruity of such formal behaviour struck her, as she took stock of her immediate surroundings, and the urge to giggle vanished.

Some day the clearing might become a smooth landing strip, but at the moment it more resembled a target for bombing practice. Giant trees had been felled to make the clearing, and the gang of men were busy extracting what was left of the huge roots, with the help of a small crawler tractor, whose engine noise was an alien intrusion on this virgin land. The tattooed stranger caught Briar's interested gaze, and said,

'We have to use dynamite to remove the roots.'

That would account for the number of enormous holes that pockmarked the ground, and made Briar wonder how long it would take to turn what looked like a disaster area into a working runway, in spite of the assistance of modern machinery.

On closer inspection, however, some order became apparent amid the chaos. Poles rammed in at intervals marked the perimeter of the area to be cleared, and to one side, clustered together, and backed under the shade of the trees, was a collection of huts. They stood high off the ground, on stilts, and were obviously the homes of the construction workers, probably built by their occupiers from the felled wood, and covered with a stout thatch of leaves to withstand the nightly tropical showers.

All round this evidence of human activity brooded the dark edge of the jungle, its presence a sombre threat that watched and waited for the opportunity to reclaim its own, and engulf in a season the work that had taken these puny interlopers so much effort to achieve.

It was into this seemingly impenetrable mass of vegetation that Drew had gone this morning. Upriver, the stranger said. Which must mean higher up the mountainside, into even thicker jungle.

Alarm thrilled through Briar. What if Drew did not return today? Or even for several days? Or not at all? In the jungle, it would be easy to get lost, or have an accident...

He strode into the clearing tall, lean, and very much alive.

One minute there was nothing in view but the dark barrier of green. The next, Drew was there, outlined against the trees. His bush shirt was dark with perspiration, his hair damp, and tossed back from his forehead, which creased in a frown as he caught sight of Briar. He stopped short, shock, consternation, and swift anger running like the rumblings of a tropical storm across his tanned features.

'What the blazes are you doing here?' he barked.

Briar had the answer to her question with a vengeance. Her presence was the reverse of welcome! Drew made no attempt to hide his displeasure at her appearance.

'I've come to deliver a letter,' she began. Said here, like that, her explanation sounded unbelievably feeble. The words died back in her throat, and Drew threw at her incredulously,

'All this way, to deliver a letter?'

His tone said he was having difficulty in taking in what he heard. His eyes raked her from top to toe, disbelieving what they saw. Briar stiffened, and erupted into speech.

'You might at least take it, now I've gone to all this trouble to bring it to you!' she flashed, and held out the letter towards him.

The delicately tinted hotel stationery, mark of a civilisation that seemed a million miles away from this savage place, dangled like a challenge between them, a gauntlet ready to be tossed down and taken up, and their glances clashed like drawn swords above it.

'It's important,' Briar insisted, when Drew made no move to take it, and slowly his hand rose and removed it from her fingers, but, instead of opening it, he stuffed it into his pocket without so much as a glance, and asked tersely,

'Who brought you here?'

'I don't know the name of the pilot. Perhaps...?' She turned to ask the tattooed man, but with typical Asian courtesy he had removed himself to some distance, in order to allow herself and Drew privacy in which to speak together. 'He wore a turban,' was the only identification she could think of.

'Ranjit,' Drew diagnosed.

His grim look made Briar cut in hastily, 'It isn't his fault I'm here. I asked him to bring me. I was silly enough to think you might be glad to...' she nearly said, 'see me,' and altered it hastily to '...to get Elizabeth's letter. She said it was important you had it as soon as possible.'

'Nothing could be important enough to bring you into malaria-infested jungle, unprotected,' Drew cut her short. 'You heard what I said to Tim.'

Briar had heard, but she had forgotten. But no matter. 'I won't be here long enough for the mosquitoes to get a chance to bite me,' she declared airily. 'The pilot's picking me up on his way back.'

'Which will be at least a week from now, if not longer.'

It took a stunned minute for the sense of what Drew said to sink in. A minute of speaking silence, which Briar broke with a dismayed, 'Did you say a *week*?'

'Maybe longer, if Ranjit gets delayed on his way back.'

'He didn't tell me,' Briar got out in a strangled voice.

'You must have had some idea yourself—or given him reason to believe you knew. Otherwise Ranjit wouldn't have consented to bring you.' Drew exonerated the pilot and put the blame squarely on Briar's shoulders, where, guiltily, she knew it belonged.

She had told the pilot she was Drew's personal assistant, which was enough to imply that she was *au fait* with all the workings of the airfield project, even to the timing of routine flights. She said faintly, 'I can't possibly stay here for a whole week.'

'You haven't got any option.'

'Surely you can contact the pilot, and ask him to come back for me?'

'Impossible. We're on a tight schedule, taking supplies to the other islands. He hasn't got the time or the fuel to waste to ferry casual sightseers about.'

He reduced her to the level of a nosy tourist, and Briar drew in a sharp breath, but before she could retort a soft Malay voice broke in.

'I'll get the men to run up a *pondok* next to yours, Drew, if you like?'

The tattooed man rejoined them, in the nick of time to defuse a threatened explosion, and Drew digressed with suave self-control, 'You've already met Lan. We work in tandem—he's in charge of the construction side of the project.'

'Drew manages the technical side,' Lan finished for him with a smile, and Briar decided waspishly that it was an appropriate division of responsibilities. Lan managed the human side, while Drew was in charge of the steel. In spite of the construction engineer's colourful tattoos, the smile behind them was warm and kind, in complete contrast to Drew's harsh unwelcome.

Drew turned to his opposite number to complete the introduction. 'This is...' He paused, deliberately, and his glance slewed to Briar, taunting her, questioning how she had described herself to the pilot. As his wife? His girlfriend?

A mixture of anger and humiliation drained the colour from Briar's cheeks, then anger won, and her return glare hated Drew. Gone was the kindly man who had shown his small nephew the delights of tourist Singapore. Here, in this primeval place, was a totally different being, one who fitted like a chameleon into his surroundings, and drew from them his cruelty, and Briar detested it, and him, as well as her own taut nerves that waited with shrinking apprehension to know how Drew would choose to describe her.

'This is...Briar,' he said, and threw a derisive look at her that read her tension, and knew the cause, and intended to extract an answer from her when it suited him.

'Don't worry, Briar.' Lan spoke, and with an effort she turned her attention back to the other man. 'We'll fix up something for you while you're here.'

As if in a dream she shook the construction engineer's outstretched hand, while she wondered raggedly just what the word worry encompassed. Was it a roof over her head, as Lan supposed? Or was it a more potent mixture of virile good looks, enhanced by carelessly flicked-back hair, damp from his jungle trip, and which made Drew look so unlike the perfectly groomed business man she was used to, oddly vulnerable, like Tim when he had just emerged from his bath. Briar dragged her eyes away. The jungle was making her fanciful.

Drew's next words jerked her back to reality. 'There's no need to waste time building another *pondok*,' he told Lan. 'Briar can share mine.' He intercepted her startled look. 'It's double the usual size, so I use one side of it as an office. I can move my things across to my own sleeping quarters, and you can occupy the rest.

This was the second time Drew had moved quarters to oblige her, but this time it was different. Was he being accommodating, as last time, or was this a piece of blatant opportunism? She had cause to know that he was quick to turn any situation to his own advantage. The silence stretched between them. Briar was acutely aware of Drew's eyes on her face, reading the expressions which flitted across her mobile features, basely betraying her thoughts.

'There's a rattan screen between us,' he jeered softly, interpreting them with devastating accuracy.

Briar felt her cheeks warm. Her eyes flew upwards to meet his, and read the derision there, and, while she loathed him for it, she knew, helplessly, that there was absolutely nothing she could do about it. She knew—and he knew—that her impulsive action had put her completely at his mercy.

'This way.' Drew's gesticulating arm was an invitation, his polite half-bow a mockery, and speechlessly Briar turned to follow him.

He came to a halt in front of a long building, which she had not noticed before. It lay further back from those occupied by the construction crew, and justified Drew's description of double. Another shelter of a similar size stood nearby, and she guessed correctly that this must belong to Lan.

A wide open veranda lay the full length of the structure, but how to reach it posed a question. This building, like the rest, stood on stilts at least eight or nine feet above the ground. Briar's eyes searched in vain for some steps up which to mount, but none presented themselves. Defeated, she turned to Drew. He stood regarding her, enjoying her dilemma, she realised vexedly.

'Where's the lift?' She felt proud of her flippancy, hiding the churning nerves in her stomach.

'There's one at each side, so you'll have your own private entrance.' He indicated a slender sapling pole, deeply notched at intervals, which rose steeply from the ground to the floor of the veranda above.

'Unfortunately there's no electricity laid on, so it isn't running,' he mocked.

Briar eyed the novel walkway in dismay. 'You can't expect me to climb up that thing?'

'There isn't any other way up.'

The pole was no more than ten inches across, and under Briar's alarmed gaze it visibly shrank. She gave a hard swallow, and managed a critical, 'With all your engineering expertise, I should have thought you could come up with something a bit better than that.'

'It has to be so that wild animals can't climb up.'

'Wild animals?' The prospect had not entered her mind.

'Wild boar, mostly.'

She had read somewhere that wild boar were reputed to be among the most savage of all the wild animals. If Drew wanted to frighten her into athletic prowess, he had passed with honours. The prospect of aggressive, marauding pigs galvanised Briar towards the foot of the pole.

'I'm not much good at balancing. I shall probably fall off.'

'Go up it on all fours, if you feel safer that way. I'll come behind you, to steady you if necessary.'

Gingerly Briar leaned forward and placed both her hands on the pole in front of her, before she allowed her feet to follow. Her all-fours position made her feel a lot more secure, but it had the disadvantage of presenting her derrière to Drew, coming up behind her.

She was vividly conscious of her slenderly cut trousers, stretched tight by bending, and her haste to return to an upright stance was nearly her undoing. She scrambled upwards, and the slender pole bent under her. She stopped, and gripped it hard, longing to shut her eyes. A cautious peep said it was a long way to the ground.

'Take it slowly,' Drew advised from just behind her, and Briar clenched her teeth at the amusement in his voice, which said he appreciated the view from where he stood, and knew it was that which had caused her unseemly haste.

It was a hundred miles up to the veranda floor. Briar clawed her way on to its flat safety with a gasp of relief, and swung to face Drew as he stepped lithely to join her, his hands in his pockets, supremely confident of his own perfect balance.

She scowled at the grin that hovered over his lips at her expense, but all he said was, 'I'll give you a hammock and a mosquito net. You can sleep this end.'

The surface of the logs, lashed together with rattan strips, had been hacked into a reasonably flat surface, with sufficient width left betwen each one to allow a cooling passage of air, and Briar looked round her curiously at this crude shelter, which was home to Drew on site.

It was spartan, without a single unnecessary trimming, as lean and clean-cut as its occupant. An offcut of a tree trunk, pushed close to a bench, served as a basic desk and stool. Briar looked in vain for the rattan screen which Drew said divided the two halves of the platform. He intercepted her glance and drawled,

'It's tied up to the roof timbers during the day.'

Her lips thinned as her colour rose, but before she could retort he added, 'Once I've moved my paperwork to the other end, the screen can remain permanently down.'

'I don't intend to stay here permanently.'

'I don't intend to let you.'

Stalemate! It was always Drew who had the last word, Briar fumed, as she watched him bend to roll the log stool to the other end of the long veranda, then come back for the heavy bench. He dragged it across the floor to join the stool, the muscles of his arms standing out like whipcord as he manoeuvred the legs of the heavy bench along the smoothest part of the logs underneath it, so that they did not snag in the gaps.

When he had placed it to his liking, Drew raised his head. 'That's your sleeping quarters fixed. Now I'll go and see if there are any clothes in the stores that might fit you.' His look assessed her size, and Briar stiffened, and, noticing, he added coolly, 'You'll need something else to put on while you wash out your smalls.'

'I won't need extra clothes—I've got some with me.' Thankfully Briar remembered her neglected shopping, still in her shoulder-bag. What a blessing she had forgotten to put it in her wardrobe at the hotel! In this, at least, she could be independent of Drew.

'You've brought some clothes with you?' His tone became glacial, but she was too relieved at having spares with her to notice anything amiss.

'In my shoulder-bag,' she confirmed, and pulled out her parcel, still encased in its wrapping. In her haste to display her self-sufficiency, she dropped the bag on to the veranda floor, and as she grabbed at it to prevent the contents from disappearing through the gaps in the logs the shopping spilled into view.

Scarlet with embarrassment, she bent to retrieve the intimate lace objects, but Drew got there first. With a swift pounce he bunched her precious bargains in one hand, as if he was bunching wastepaper, and drove Briar to protest,

'Don't screw them up like that—you'll crease them!'

'You said you believed the pilot would be coming back to collect you the same day?'

'Yes, of course I did.' The ice registered, and it brought Briar's gaze up abruptly to his face. Shocked, she found herself engulfed in a freezing anger which turned Drew's eyes almost as black as his thunderous scowl.

'Do you expect me to believe that?' he snarled.

'Believe what, for goodness' sake?'

'You, when you said you expected to go back to Singapore today. Yet you come ready equipped with several changes of clothing.'

'I forgot to put them in the wardrobe at the hotel. Elizabeth and I went shopping.'

'You went shopping together days ago, the day after Elizabeth arrived.'

'We went shopping together yesterday. She wanted some things for their holiday in Thailand.'

'What holiday in Thailand? Is that just another excuse for you to desert your post? I told you to stay on, for Tim's sake.'

'There's no post to desert any longer. Robert arrived after you left, and he's taken Elizabeth and Tim on a holiday to Thailand for a whole month— as he's got every right to do. If you'd stop shouting at me for a few minutes, and read the letter, it explains everything. You're making the workmen stare at me as if I'm some sort of apparition!'

'They're not used to camp-followers.'

'How *dare* you?'

Briar's hand came up in a cat's-paw slap, aimed at Drew's face, but his fingers rose with equal speed and fielded the blow before it could connect. They circled Briar's slender wrist with crushing force.

'Try that again,' he gritted, 'and I might just forget I'm a gentleman.'

'You're a beast!' she choked, on threatening tears.

'You say that now,' Drew jeered, 'but you were willing to take a chance on it when you packed your bag and came along. Did you think to put in a sarong as well?'

'A sarong? No, why should I?' The sheer unexpectedness of the question stopped Briar's stormy rejoinder.

'You're going to need one while you're here.'

'I'll wear my own clothes, thanks.' Her chin came up. 'Sarongs aren't my scene. They don't match my lifestyle back home.'

'Whatever your lifestyle elsewhere, while you're here, whenever you dress, undress, or take a bath, you'll do so under the decent privacy of a sarong. It may have escaped your notice, but the *pondoks* don't have doors.' Drew gestured towards the leaf-thatched roofs and open-to-view living quarters of the crude dwellings nearby. 'You're the only woman, in a camp that hasn't seen one for months.'

'I told you, I don't have a sarong.'

'I've got one you can use.'

Drew reached down and unzipped the canvas holdall which Briar recognised as the one he had taken with him from the hotel. He pulled out a long length of brightly coloured cotton cloth and thrust it into her hands.

'Use this.'

She regarded it with unwilling interest. The attractively batik-patterned fabric was of good quality, and beautifully coloured. Her investigating fingers told her that the material was new; it still retained its stiff dressing. What had brought such a garment into Drew's possession? Who had he had in mind when he purchased it? Briar thrust the question aside. The answer might be enlightening, but it was not her business. To keep the question at bay, she concentrated on more immediate matters.

'Tell me where the bathroom is.'

In the air-conditioned comfort of the hotel in Singapore, the enervating heat had not affected her unduly, but, lacking such luxury, the jungle humidity bathed her in a clammy embrace that made her long for a shower and a change of clothes.

'There isn't one,' said Drew. 'You bathe in the river.'

Briar's eyes widened, but she refused to give him the satisfaction of knowing what it cost her to shrug and return lightly, 'Then tell me how to get there.'

Drew slanted her an enigmatic look that sent an icy trickle down her spine and he drawled, 'The bathing pool is a hundred yards or so along the track. But if you imagine I'm going to let you wander about the jungle on your own you can forget it. It's only too easy to get lost, and I haven't got the time to waste rounding you up if you do. I'll take you there myself, and wait for you. So be quick about your bath, and don't waste any time wallowing.'

CHAPTER SIX

CHANGED and refreshed, Briar was able, later, to view her baptism in jungle bathroom etiquette with wry amusement.

Drew led her through the dark fringe of trees, at the spot where he himself had emerged, and along a narrow track which had not been obvious to Briar from the clearing.

They walked in single file, which was all the room the track allowed them, amid a gloomy twilight, cut off from the sunshine by the thick green canopy high over their heads.

Drew commanded, 'Keep close behind me. Don't lag behind, or you might take the wrong turning and get lost.'

His command was unnecessary, for Briar had no intention of allowing him out of her sight. Dense undergrowth foreshortened her view to a mere few yards ahead, underlying his warning, and the prospect of wild boar roaming in the thickets on either side was sufficient to glue her to his heels.

She was forced to accelerate into a trot to keep up with him. His longer stride carried him forward at an easy lope, which she had difficulty in matching, and in the end she was forced to gasp,

'Slow down, for pity's sake! I'm absolutely melting!'

'You should have stayed in Singapore.'

He threw her an unsympathetic glance over his shoulder, but he slowed his pace a little, nevertheless, and it allowed her to keep up with him more easily. After another few yards of stumbling progress, in which she was torn between keeping her eyes on Drew and the need to watch her every step in case she might trip on one of the multitude of exposed tree roots that lay in wait for unwary feet, Drew announced to her relief,

'Only a few more yards to go. You can hear the falls from here.'

How deliciously cool they sounded!

The splash of falling water added another dimension to the mysterious orchestra of grunts, whistles, chatters and squeals which emanated from unidentified throats all round her, and made Briar feel even more of an intruder in this alien world into which she had so impulsively ventured.

Abruptly Drew veered off to one side, and as the greenery closed behind him Briar realised with a shiver that if she had not been watching him carefully she would have no idea which way he had gone.

A branch still swung slightly, identifying his route, and she ducked under it and found herself standing at the top of a steep bank. Drew was waiting for her, his hand outstretched.

'I can manage,' she said, and he took as little notice this time as he had when he had lifted her down from the trishaw. He grasped her firmly by both arms and eased her down beside him until the bank flattened out. He released her, then, and Briar had to resist an urge to rub the now familiar tingles that spread along her arms from where his fingers had rested.

He said, 'I can't afford to let you risk an accident. We haven't got any doctors on tap out here, and it disrupts the pilot's routine if we have to call him in for emergencies.'

Nothing and nobody must stand in the way of Drew's precious work. He had no right to criticise Robert for being a workaholic, Briar thought—then forgot her ire in quick delight as Drew moved to one side to allow her to view the scene in front of her.

The river chattered over low boulders. It washed the edge of a narrow shingle beach and cascaded in a cloud of white spray across a rocky ledge, dropping several feet into a small pool. She gazed enchanted.

'It's absolutely lovely!'

'All mod cons,' murmured Drew, and added, 'I'll wait for you on the path at the top of the bank. Sing out if anything scares you—or if you want your back scrubbed.'

His low laugh taunted her as he retreated through the undergrowth, and Briar flung him a vitriolic glare, which was wasted because he was already out of sight.

The effect Drew was having on her was beginning to scare her more than somewhat. She waited for several tense minutes, in order to give him time to get right to the top of the bank, where she knew the waters of the pool would be out of sight. She had no way of knowing that Drew would keep his promise. His silent tread gave her no clue as to his actual whereabouts, but the greenery through which he had disappeared had stopped swinging, giving no indication that he might be lurking in its depths.

Briar shrugged. If Drew decided to play Peeping Tom, there was absolutely nothing she could do to prevent him. The sarong looked completely inadequate as a shelter, but she desperately wanted a bath. She draped the length of cotton cloth about her, and wriggling out of her clothes, stepped into the river, carrying the sarong with her.

Immediately the brisk flow of the current caught at the material and tried to snatch it from her grasp. Panic-stricken, she grabbed at the ends, and succeeded in wrapping it back around her. The hunted look she directed towards the bank told her nothing. The thick canopy of green looked back, hiding its secrets, and, reassured, she waded further into the water, until she was safely covered up to her shoulders and could allow the sarong to float freely from where she had knotted the end around one arm, while she soaped away the day's travel stains.

It was bliss to allow the cool water to lave away the sticky heat, and a bona fide starred hotel could not have provided a more welcome bath. She laughed as a shoal of small fish swam round her, curious to investigate the bubbles of lather floating on the surface, from the tablet of soap Drew had given her, then dipped her face beneath the water, to watch a small river turtle scuttle away from beneath her bare feet.

She closed her eyes, and lifted her face to allow the waterfall to shower the soap from her curls, a slender statuette swathed in bright cotton, its now soaking folds clinging to her slight figure and outlining its perfection as it could not possibly do when the material was dry.

In the sensuous pleasure of feeling clean and cool again, Briar forgot the time, and started when a disembodied voice hailed her from the trees.

'I'll give you just five more minutes to get dressed, then I'm coming to fetch you!'

The ultimatum shocked Briar back to her surroundings. In her haste to be out of the water and into her clothes, she stumbled and lost her footing, and the swift current carried her several yards downstream before her strong young arms were able to turn her about and swim back again to the safety of the shingle bank.

How many minutes of the five had her swim wasted? she wondered nervously. There was no means of knowing, and her fingers became all thumbs with haste, as she grabbed for the small pile of clothing awaiting her above the water level.

'Ugh!' She dropped the first garment hastily, and the voice, much closer now, called,

'What's the matter?'

'My clothes. They're covered with creepy-crawlies!'

'Give them a hard shake. Make sure there aren't any insects left inside before you put them on, or you might get stung in unmentionable places.'

With shuddery aversion Briar shook and turned, and shook again, and discovered the wet sarong was even more unmanageable when she finally began to dress than when she had reversed the process under its dry folds.

'Are you ready yet?'

'No. Wait a minute.'

'I've waited long enough. It's suppertime, and I'm hungry. I'm coming in.'

A rustle sounded, disconcertingly close. Branches swayed. Desperately, Briar pushed reluctant buttons into equally reluctant buttonholes, fiercely condemning their lack of co-operation under her breath, as a bush on the very edge of the forest bent under the force of a thrusting arm.

She wrung drips from her curls with painful haste, but when Drew rounded the bush and stood on the shingle bank alongside her she was able to turn and face him without loss of dignity.

His eyes raked her from top to toe, reading her haste from her still rumpled shirt, with the buttons mated to the wrong buttonholes, and a grin hovered over his lips, but although Briar tensed herself for a sharp retort, he made no comment, merely inviting her, 'Let's go and eat.'

Conversation became easier back at the *pondok*, where darkness made a neutral ground between them, and Briar stepped on to it cautiously.

'I'm eating your stores,' she realised guiltily.

There was boiled rice and fish, and fresh pineapple, which Drew sliced from a whole new fruit and handed to her in manageable pieces to assuage her hunger and thirst at the same time.

'We live off the land here, not off stores. There's an abundance of wild deer and pig in the forest, and fish in the rivers, and plenty of wild fruit for the picking. If we need more, the longhouse village upriver trades with us for salt and sugar. The pineapples come from them—they grow them farther up the mountain. Have some more?'

Briar hesitated, and Drew urged, 'It won't keep. Once anything's cut here it goes rotten within a day. That applies to human flesh too, so if you cut yourself even slightly don't ignore it. Come to me and have it properly dressed and disinfected.'

'I heal without any trouble.'

'Nobody heals without trouble in the jungle, and wounds quickly turn gangrenous. Blood poisoning can set in from even a tiny scratch. Bear that in mind, and don't take any risks. I can't afford sickness in camp.'

The risk for Drew would be in delaying his airstrip, Briar reasoned cynically, but, bathed and fed, and leaning back in the canvas chair which Drew had produced from somewhere for her, she felt disinclined to argue.

Lethargy overtook her as the day exacted its toll, but although her body felt limp her mind remained vividly alive. It was as if the wild alertness of the jungle creatures communicated itself to her, stripping away the thin veneer of Western sophistication and giving her a heightened sensitivity that made her more aware of her surroundings, of the significance of every slight sound, and the meaning of each silence.

Acutely aware of Drew.

She knew, without needing to turn her head to look at him, that he was leaning back in an attitude of total relaxation, reminiscent of one of the large jungle cats, limp with ease, and yet with coiled-spring muscles ready to tense into instant action should the need arise.

A low murmur of talk, and an occasional burst of laughter, came from the huts where the construction crew were gathered for their own evening meal, and, as if the social sounds prompted him to a similar effort of conversation, Drew enquired,

'Have you been out east before?'

'Only once, and never this far east. We—I visited India.'

Briar corrected the 'we' and wondered if Drew had noticed, but his casual, 'On holiday?' gave no hint.

'Yes.' The monosyllable sounded terse and uncommunicative, and reluctantly Briar padded it out with, 'To Delhi, actually, and a flying visit over the border into Kashmir.'

She and Philip had spent their honeymoon in India, and Briar did not want to be reminded of it. To turn the conversation away from things eastern, she offered, 'Most of my travelling has been done in Europe and America. I spent quite a lot of time in both, on exchange study courses.'

'Studying what?'

'Remedial therapy—the art of getting people back on their feet again after horrendous accidents.'

Briar did not mind enlarging on that subject. It was safely pre-Philip.

Drew drawled, 'From being a professional therapist to acting as a jack-of-all-trades for your brother seems a bit of a let-down,' and jerked Briar back to the realisation that no subject was safe with him.

She answered defensively, 'Tony needed my help.'

'Surely not to the extent of breaking up your career? Therapists in that kind of specialist field can't be exactly ten a penny, whereas I should say that your brother would be able to train anyone with reasonable intelligence, in a fairly short period of time, to do the job he required.'

Whatever Drew might or might not say, Briar felt that she herself had already said too much, if it meant having to fend off questions about her personal life. She discouraged further ones with a flat, 'I'm in between jobs at the moment, so it was convenient for both of us.'

In between being a wife and a mother, and...what next? The patter of the first night shower on the broad jungle leaves gave her no answer, and Briar stirred restlessly, her unconscious sigh echoing that of the wind in the branches.

Slight though the sound was, Drew's keen ears diagnosed its source, and immediately he uncoiled his long frame and rose to his feet with the lazy grace that again reminded Briar of one of the big jungle cats.

'You're tired,' he said. 'I'll sling your hammock for you.' When he had roped it securely to the roof beams, he warned, 'Don't forget to tuck the mosquito net well in. Did you take those anti-malaria tablets I gave you?' At her nod, he approved, 'Good. The skeeters in this part of the world are savage little brutes, and your nice English rose complexion looks very tempting.'

Tempting to the mosquitos, or to Drew? Briar's eyes searched his face, trying to read its expression through the dancing shadows shed by the flames of the cooking fires from the quarters of the construction crew. He stood for a moment, looking down at her, as if he was waiting for something, but the shadows defeated her, and she could not tell what it might be.

After a long silence Drew said, 'Now for the rattan screen.'

He reached up and tugged loose the cord holding it to the roof, and the screen tumbled to its full length, with Drew and herself both on his side of the barrier, and out of sight from the other huts.

'Goodnight, Briar,' he murmured, and took what he had been waiting for.

His kiss was long and unhurried, and his mouth imprisoned her lips with a masterful force, holding all the promise and the subtle threat of the dark jungle night. His head became a part of the darkness above her, and his hands gripped her shoulders with a steel strength that pressed her against him, and, too surprised to resist, Briar felt a heat scorch through her veins that owed nothing to being so close to the Equator, and everything to being much too close to Drew.

'Goodnight, Briar,' he repeated softly, and released her.

She stumbled back against the rattan screen, which instantly billowed inwards, offering her no support, and Drew bent swiftly and lifted the bottom of it and dropped it over her head, so that it came in between them, hiding him from view. But not from her hearing.

'Sleep tight,' filtered through it, and Briar did not need to see the expression on his face to read the mockery there.

'*You...*' she breathed furiously, then went deathly still as a burst of laughter from the construction crew's quarters warned her that she was within their sight and hearing, if they should choose to look and listen.

Controlling her urge to retaliate as best she might, she performed the contortions necessary under the now nearly dry sarong to enable her to roll into the hammock, and tuck the mosquito net protectively round her against the invading swarms. Their frustrated whining made a plaintive background music to other stealthy night sounds, coming from furtive movements among the nearby thickets, which made Briar thankful that Drew was close to hand.

The pure, high notes of a bamboo flute, expertly played, pierced the darkness, then died away as the performer too sought his sleeping mat, and the steadily increasing downpour, which had earlier doused the tiny pricks of light from a myriad fireflies, now damped down the cooking fires until they became no more than a fading glow.

With nothing on which to focus her thoughts, they drifted to India, and Philip, and Lucy, but refused to remain with any one of them, and latched on to Drew instead, and it was Drew who haunted her dreams, jeering, 'Camp-follower!' while he hurried ahead of her along an endless jungle path, much too fast to enable her to keep up with him, and cruelly ignored her shouted pleas to, 'Wait for me. Please, don't leave me,' as he ducked out of sight among the leaves and left her alone, and feeling desperately afraid.

The shouts were real.

Briar sat bolt upright, shocked into wakefulness by she knew not what. What was happening? Where was she? The hammock rocked alarmingly under her sudden movement, threatening to deposit her on the floor, and she grabbed at the rope sides, waiting for it to steady, as memory returned with growing consciousness.

Her alarmed ears caught another shout, and then another, as a burst of furious yelling echoed across the clearing, suggesting pitched battle, followed by two loud bangs. Figures ran to and fro, holding aloft tarred rope torches. The reek of tar drifted back in a choking cloud across the veranda.

Someone was trying to set light to the *pondoks*!

Frantically Briar clawed herself free from the mosquito net, heedless of the swinging hammock, which retaliated by depositing her on the floor with a force that jarred her teeth together.

'Drew!' Her voice was a thin thread of horror, but no answer came to reassure her from the other side of the rattan screen. Urgently, she tried again. *'Drew!'*

Silence mocked her, and Briar froze in the crouch where she had landed, trying to make herself as inconspicuous as possible, as she watched the torches waving to and fro, lending a bizarre light to the confusion in the clearing.

The tarry-smelling smoke filled her nostrils and caught at her throat, making her want to cough, and hurriedly she put her hand to her mouth to stifle the sound, fearful of drawing attention to her presence.

Nervously she recalled Drew's harsh, 'You're the only woman in a camp that hasn't seen one for months.' Where was Drew? What was happening?

The crazily milling torches sorted themselves into some kind of order, and Briar gave a sob of relief as she realised that their bearers were running away from the *pondoks*, and not towards them. They came to a halt at the compound which housed the construction machinery, that precious aid without which the landing strip could not be completed, and the guttering light illumined a scene of furiously fighting figures, reminiscent of a Hollywood movie.

Except that this was not fiction. It was terrifyingly real. Horror gripped Briar as she watched the struggling bodies. Why did not Drew come to her? Where was he? Was he safe, or was he...?

Still crouched low on the veranda floor, she froze with fear, not for herself, but for Drew. She did not question the extremity of her fear, which held her body rigid, while her eyes winged frantically through the noisy darkness, seeking in vain for a sight of the missing engineer.

So engrossed was she in the terrifying scene in front of her that she did not feel the slight shake of the veranda, as running feet took the notched pole stairway of the *pondok* at top speed. A heavily tattooed face appeared without warning over the edge of the veranda floor, directly on a level with her own, and, shocked back to her own peril, Briar recoiled with a suppressed scream.

'Don't be frightened—it's only me,' Lan called out, and joined her on the veranda with an agile bound. 'Drew sent me back for his pistol, and to make sure you were safe.'

He had sent Lan. He had not come himself. Briar pushed aside an inner pang and demanded, 'What's going on, Lan? Where's Drew?'

She found herself talking to the rattan screen. Lan was already on its other side, searching among Drew's possessions for the pistol. He reappeared, holding it purposefully in one hand, and answered,

'The last I saw of Drew, he was right in the thick of the fray, and giving a very good account of himself. He was taking on two for everyone else's one. I'm glad he's on our side,' he added with feeling.

'Lan, *please*! Tell me what's going *on*!'

'Bandits,' Drew's opposite number said succinctly, and made Briar almost wish she had not asked. 'They're losing their taste for the raid now, though, thanks to Drew,' he hastened to reassure her. 'This should help to send them packing.'

He did something with the pistol, and, raising his hand, pointed it over the edge of the veranda towards where the fighting was the thickest. Briar gave a terrified cry. 'Be careful! You might hit anybody.' He might hit Drew. How could he tell who was which, amid such confusion?

She longed to close her eyes as Lan pulled the trigger, but instead of the loud explosion she expected there was only a muffled plop! and then an exploding flare flooded the clearing with brilliant light.

For a brief second the contestants froze as the light arced skywards, illuminating every small corner of the arena, and clearly identifying friend from foe. The flare faded, Lan shot another one to follow the first, and the tableau broke up in wild disorder.

Running figures made for the cover of the jungle and disappeared amid the green, and others ran in their wake, until a whistle shrilled, calling the pursuers to order and bringing them back reluctantly to assemble in the compound, where after what appeared to be a brief council of war a few remained behind on guard, while the rest streamed back towards the *pondoks*, chattering excitedly.

The pole stairway rocked again, and another face appeared above the veranda floor. Briar jumped to her feet with a relieved cry.

'Drew!'

Her greeting choked back in her throat. For a wild, hysterical moment she thought, he's had his face tattooed, just like Lan. But this was no artistic scroll and leaf pattern, painfully executed by a craftsman. Instead, streaks of tarry soot mingled with ominous rivulets of red, running from a welling cut on his forehead that was already matting his hair, and spreading down across his cheeks. Briar felt sick. Like a knell, Drew's own words of warning came back to her.

'... blood poisoning can set in from even a tiny scratch... Wounds quickly turn gangrenous.' She remembered the shine of torchlight on steel, and shuddered.

'Drew! Oh, Drew,' she breathed, and ran towards him.

'Keep down, out of sight, until the raiders are clear of the camp.' His snarled rebuff rocked her back on her heels. 'You being in camp has given me problems enough, without adding to them by getting yourself kidnapped and held to ransom by a bunch of ne'er-do-wells,' he snapped.

Reaction from an extremity of fear brewed quick anger, and Briar snapped, 'You talk as if the jungle is the sole property of men!' The arrogance of it! 'There must be women in the villages.'

'The women in the jungle villages belong here.'

And she did not. Briar fought back from the slap-down. 'You needn't concern yourself on my behalf. If I was kidnapped, I wouldn't come begging to you to bail me out!'

'You'd have to wait for a long time if you did.'

A moment ago she had been fearing for Drew's life. Now they were quarrelling. Briar felt torn between an angry desire to hit him, and a humiliating desire to cry. Pride chose the former.

'Nice to know how much I'm worth!' she struck out verbally. She had been worth less than nothing to Philip, and it seemed as if her valuation was equally low in this man's eyes, and the bitterness showed. It narrowed Drew's gaze on her face, reading the compressed lips and the strained line of the delicate jaw that betrayed teeth clenched tight against tears. He said, more quietly,

'The price the villains would ask wouldn't be in cash.'

'What else is there?'

She did not care, but conversation helped to keep at bay the threatened loss of self-control.

'They'd try to force us to abandon building the airstrips on the islands, with all the deprivation that would mean to their inhabitants.'

His answer surprised from her a shocked, 'Abandon the prospect of a flying doctor service? They must be mad!'

'They have their reasons.'

'Their reasons can wait.' Professionalism overcame her ire. 'You're bleeding quite badly— I'll dress the cuts for you.'

'I'll attend to them myself,' Drew refused, and swayed dizzily on his feet.

'Let Briar do it,' Lan intervened. 'That is, if she can stand the sight of so much blood.'

'I've dealt with worse. Tell me where you keep your first-aid kit.'

Briar hoped her brisk tone hid the twisted knot that had become her stomach. She had seen many worse injuries, but none of them borne by Drew, and always before the initial cleaning-up process had already been coped with by medics. Here she was on her own, without any back-up, and probably with only primitive equipment.

Lan proved her estimate of the camp stores to be a rank injustice. 'Bandages, dressings, penicillin, sterilised water.' He quickly produced amenities that would not disgrace the accident unit of a cottage hospital back home, and pressed Drew down on to the camp chair with a stern,

'Sit down before you fall down, and be thankful Briar's willing to help.'

She threw the tattooed man a grateful look. At least one person was glad of her presence in the camp. She bent to inspect the medical equipment, and asked over her shoulder, 'Are any of the crew injured?'

'Don't worry about the crew. I'll attend to them,' Lan assured her, and disappeared down the notched pole to carry out his own inspection of his men.

Left alone, Briar worked swiftly, and in silence. First of all she bathed Drew's face, washing away the blood and streaks of tarry soot, and was relieved to discover that underneath there was unmarked skin, with only the one wound on Drew's forehead to worry about.

That was bad enough, in all conscience. Briar steeled herself to examine it. It proved to be long and deep, but it was a clear cut, with no jagged edges to make healing difficult. She guessed correctly that the flash of steel she had seen in the torchlight was the blow which had been responsible.

Carefully she used the sterilised water to irrigate the cut, and pressed on a penicillin dressing to stem the flow of blood, willing her fingers not to tremble, and a hovering faintness not to overwhelm her.

While she worked, Drew leaned back in the chair with his eyes closed, whether from reaction to the loss of blood, or to prevent the water from getting into his eyes when she washed his face, she could not tell.

The white dressing stood out in stark contrast to his dark hair, and his face reflected its pallor in the guttering light from the rope torch which Lan had left fixed to one of the veranda uprights, to enable her to see more clearly what she was doing.

Briar frowned anxiously as she bent to finger a dark, wet lock of hair that persisted in dropping over the bandage. Drew's hair was thick and strong, as virile as its owner. And just as stubborn, Briar decided vexedly, as the wave flopped back again, forcing her to repeat the process, and endure once more the strange, electric sensation that shot through her fingers when she touched it, and travelled the length of her arm. It made her want to snatch her hand away, and at the same time gave her an errant longing to continue to run her fingers through his hair, and experience more of the mixed pain and pleasure that was as bewildering as were her own mixed-up feelings.

'I haven't had my face washed for me since I was Tim's age,' Drew murmured, and Briar gasped.

His eyes were wide open, and watching her with undisguised amusement and something else which in the uncertain torchlight she found impossible to define. She had been too preoccupied to notice, and now she did, her own cheeks flushed bright scarlet and she snatched her hand away from his hair, as if her fingers had indeed encountered a real electric shock.

'I . . . you . . .' she stammered, and got no further.

Drew's hands rose and closed about her waist with a strength which belied the pallor of his cheeks, and he drew her remorselessly down on to his knee and held her there.

His head bent, and his lips engulfed her own. They thanked her without words for washing away the stains of battle, and for dressing his wound so tenderly. They punished her for having the temerity to follow him into the jungle and lay on him the burden of responsibility for her safety. And then his kiss changed and deepened, forgiving her, as his lips explored the sweet, soft contours of her mouth, which parted to receive them with a willing acceptance that was outside her power to control.

She whispered, 'I was so afraid, when I saw the sword-blade flash.'

'Head-hunting has gone out of fashion nowadays.' Hungrily Drew took possession of her lips again. 'Mine is still firmly on my shoulders,' he teased. 'Feel for yourself.'

He guided her hands round his neck, where her fingertips encountered the crisp, short ends of his neatly barbered hairline.

Philip had worn his hair long, yuppie-style—much longer than her own. Briar had teased him about it, tried to persuade him to have it cut shorter, because privately she thought it made him look effeminate, but he had resisted all her efforts to make him wear it less than shoulder length, claiming the style made him look 'sexy'.

To what end, she now knew.

Stung by the memory, Briar snatched her hands away and pressed them hard against Drew's chest, pushing herself away from him, and straining to be free from his hold.

'Let me go!' The words were choked out of her on a note of panic, and in the torchlight her eyes were wild.

'What's the matter? Don't you like being kissed?'

'No, I...' It was humiliating to find out how much she liked being kissed, by Drew. Humiliating, and dangerous. She renewed her struggles to be free.

'Loose me. The crew will see.'

'The screen's down; they can't see through that.' His arms remained a steel band round her, holding her to him, and desperately she flung back,

'I didn't come here for this. Whatever you think, I'm *not* a camp-follower!'

That unlocked his grip. His whole body stiffened, and his arms dropped to his sides as he growled, 'You know it wasn't meant in that way.'

'I don't care which way it was meant. I'm not your plaything!'

'You were enjoying yourself just as much as me, a minute ago. You can't deny it.'

Her traitorous lips, that had given back kiss for kiss, could find no words to deny it, and could only repeat, helplessly, 'I didn't come here for that.'

Drew thrust her from him impatiently. 'What did you come for, then?'

With tears coursing down her cheeks as she lay in her hammock later, listening to Drew's quiet breathing on the other side of the rattan screen, Briar refused to face the answer. In self-defence she scorned him. How like a man, to make passionate love one minute and be fast asleep the next!

From the equipment compound she could just make out the figures of the guards, moving to and fro, and behind the *pondok* the jungle brooded, silent and watchful, and in between the two Briar tossed and turned, wrestling with the turmoil of her mind.

Experience with Philip had taught her never to trust another man. It would have been more help if it had also taught her that she must not trust herself either.

Why had she followed Drew into the jungle? Bitterly she regretted the impulse that had brought her here. Until tonight she had been confident of her ability to handle her own feelings. Now she was not so sure.

The forced intimacy of washing Drew's face, and dressing his wound, had tilled a fertile soil in which the effects of his kiss took root and grew with alarming speed, and, locked in a dark jungle of Drew's planting, her turbulent thoughts raced to and fro, and could find no clear pathway to bring her out again into the light.

Lan had come back to report on the condition of his construction crew. 'A few minor cuts and bruises—nothing serious,' he'd reassured them, and answered Briar's nervous question about the bandits, 'They won't wait around, don't worry. They'll head for one of the other islands in the chain, to lick their wounds.'

Ruefully Briar wished that she could escape from herself so easily, as the swift Equatorial dawn greeted another day, and she rose unrefreshed from her hammock, feeling more weary than when she had sought its rest the night before.

CHAPTER SEVEN

LAN joined them on the veranda for breakfast.

A chill dawn mist enveloped the jungle, drifting ghostly wet fingers among the green, and making Briar grateful for the hot meal porridge which accompanied her bowl of rice and mixed vegetables.

She had already put a fresh dressing on Drew's wound, and was reassured to find no sign of infection there, and his cheeks this morning had regained their usual healthy colour, but, heavy-eyed herself from her unresolved encounter with her own emotions, she felt her spirits reflected the early morning gloom, and she was content to listen while the two men talked.

She gathered that the crew were making light of their injuries, as was Drew. 'I'm going up-river again this morning,' he decided, and Briar remembered that he had been up-river yesterday, when she arrived. Was it only yesterday? It seemed like a hundred years ago.

Drew enquired of his opposite number, 'Have you seen any signs of our visitors from last night?' and Lan shook his head.

'None at all. The guards have checked the immediate area around the camp, with no result. I've alerted the nearest villages, just to be on the safe side, and radioed the other islands to put them on their guard as well, but I think, after the lesson we gave them last night, it will be some time before they'll dare to come here again.'

'Did they cause much damage?'

'Unfortunately, yes. They've put the small crawler tractor out of action. It's a nuisance, because we've reached the stage where it's in constant use. I've called up Ranjit on the radio and asked him if he can bring forward his return trip, and fly us in some urgent spares.'

Ranjit was the helicopter pilot. Briar's ears pricked, and her spoon poised motionless over her bowl of porridge as she waited tensely for what was to come next.

What was unfortunate for Lan could turn out to be very fortunate indeed for herself. If the helicopter returned early, she would be able to fly out with it, back to Singapore, back to sanity.

Once she was safely away from this strange, exotic world, that played weird tricks with her senses—once she was away from Drew—she would become her own person again, controlled, and in control, and she would be able to laugh at her moment of weakness last night, when she'd lain in his arms and gave back kiss for kiss.

Back in her own familiar world, she would know the episode for just that— a moment of weakness, born of extremities of fear and shock, that had rocked her temporarily off balance.

'How soon can Ranjit get here?' asked Drew.

Briar waited with bated breath for Lan's reply. 'Maybe late tomorrow, or more likely the morning after.'

Another two days. The confidence of daylight said she could hold out for that long, whatever the provocation. Briar finished the rest of her breakfast with renewed appetite, and saw that the mist was lifting, rapidly dispersing with the growing heat of the sun, like an omen which suggest that she would soon see her own confused feelings disappear with equal speed.

Feeling more relaxed, she joined in the conversation. 'It seems you're inflicted with the western disease of vandals out here as well, Lan. Why should the raiders want to damage your machinery?'

'They'll go to any lengths to stop the airstrips from being completed,' Lan told her gravely. 'Once there's a regular air service to the islands, it will not only bring in medical help, but law and order as well, and that won't suit the raiders. They've had rich pickings from the villages, up to now, and because the islands are so isolated their forays have gone more or less unchecked. A regular air service will make the area easier to police.'

'Rich pickings?' Briar frowned her puzzlement. What could the raiders find to steal in simple jungle villages? Lan read the question in her face, and answered it unasked.

'The longhouse people own artefacts which are in great demand among wealthy collectors in the outside world. To the villagers, these things are just ordinary household items—jars in which they store their rice wine, and pots for everyday use. But to collectors, they're priceless. A lot of the ceramics initially found their way here from China, with the drift of population, and they've been handed down through the longhouse families for generations.

Some of them are hundreds of years old, especially the burial urns.'

'It's hard to believe that such things exist, in the middle of the jungle.'

'Nevertheless, they do. And their existence became widely known when the younger men from the villages began to drift to the coast, looking for work. They were no longer content with the old ways, and they took jobs with the oil companies. To get extra money, some of them traded their belongings, among them the rice jars.'

He smiled at the question in her eyes. 'Yes, I was one of those who went to seek my fortune. I was lucky—I was taken on by a company which was willing to give me my training, and now I've come back, to use my knowledge to benefit my own people. And to warn them, so that they've become aware of the value of their possessions. Now, of course, they refuse to sell, so the bandits are reduced to having to steal what they want. There's a ready market for their spoils on the mainland, and easy money to be had for very little risk. Up to now the villains have had a quick escape by boat to other islands after a raid, with little or no chance of retribution, but the arrival of the airstrips is changing all that.'

'I still find it hard to believe what's happened,' Briar exclaimed when Lan had gone, and Drew sent her a quizzical look.

'Did you expect to find a sanitised form of jungle here, like the so-called ''jungle trails'' on offer in the city parks?' he scorned. 'They're about as close to the real thing as the candy-floss romances in the women's magazines are true in real life.'

With an effort, Briar kept her lips tight closed. She did not need Drew to tell her that. Fictional romances all had happy endings. Abruptly she steered on to another subject.

'You mentioned you were going up-river again today. What takes you there? Another airstrip?'

'No. You'll see when we get there.'

'*We?*'

Prickles of warning tingled across her skin. To spend a day in the jungle with Drew held out a promise of excitement—and danger. Danger of a quite different kind from that posed by the raiders of the night before. The brief spell spent in Drew's arms had taught her just how vulnerable she still was.

To Drew, it was sheer opportunism. He had kissed her because she was there. For herself, another such hour could spell disaster, and for her life's sake she dared not risk reopening wounds that were as yet barely healed.

There was no way she wanted to risk spending a whole day in his company, locked away in the green solitude of the forest, without the safety net of having other people around. Impulsively she opened her mouth to make some excuse to remain in the *pondok*, but with quick intuition Drew divined her intention, and moved to forestall her.

'You can't stay here on your own. It isn't safe.'

'Lan will be here.'

'Lan will be supervising his crew. He's got better things to do than to keep an eye on you.'

Drew made no bones about her nuisance value! But, while one part of Briar smarted under his attack, another traitorous part hugged itself in secret anticipation of the day that lay ahead.

At sight of the fragile-looking dugout canoe drawn up on the river bank just above the waterfall, she objected, 'I'm not going to ride in that! It doesn't look big enough to hold two.'

'It's designed for that purpose, so get in and don't argue.'

Ignoring her protests, he lifted her firmly into the nose of the craft and pushed it out into midstream before she could jump out again, and, marooned in deep water on her own, she gasped her alarm as she felt the current tug at the canoe, sucking it towards the waterfall. She gripped the sides with both hands as Drew leapt towards it from the bank. If he missed, she would be pulled helplessly over the lip of the fall.

He landed amidships in a perfect touchdown that scarcely even rocked the craft, and, grabbing up the long metal-tipped pole which provided its motive power, he reversed the drift of the canoe and drove it upstream with strong thrusts, pitting his own strength against the mighty power of the downhill current.

Briar watched, fascinated, as his sinewy arms propelled them forward, his lithe body bending and flexing to the rhythm of his strokes, with an accustomed ease which made her wonder where he had learned the art. He explained without being asked.

'I put in a lot of practice at punting, alongside the Backs at Cambridge.'

University-educated fitted, Briar thought. She wondered which college he had attended, and, with

sharper curiosity, who had been his companion in
the punt then. Her heart did a peculiar somersault
as she tried to picture the kind of girl with whom
he had shared those far-off, halcyon summer days,
cruising along the quiet reaches of the Cam.

Had the two young students stood together
afterwards, arm in arm, on one of the famous
bridges of that lovely old city, watching the water
flow beneath their feet, and dreaming their dreams
of the future? Surely those dreams could not have
visualised such a far-flung outpost as this?

More importantly, did the girl still exist, in that
future which was now the present? And was she
waiting for Drew to return? If so, would she be
prepared to give up the career she had studied so
hard to attain, meekly deferring to Drew's dislike
of what he called 'weekend wives'?

Impatiently, Briar shook her thoughts back to
her immediate surroundings. Neither Drew's past
nor his future was anything to do with her. It was
enough that she must keep a tight hold on herself,
that he did not take control of her own present.

An hour of hard effort later, the river began to
narrow, making the use of the pole difficult. The
trees arched overhead, forming a tunnel, and Drew
slid the pole into the bottom of the canoe and
picked up a crudely shaped hook which Briar had
not noticed before. With scarcely a break in the
even flow of his movements he reached up with the
hook and gripped it on to the overhead branches,
then began to pull their craft through the water by
this new method.

Both means of progress required immense
strength to keep the canoe on course against the

adverse and fast-flowing current, but in spite of the loss of blood which he had suffered the night before Drew appeared unperturbed by his efforts, merely remarking,

'It's easier going back. We freewheel downhill.'

'Balang! Balang!'

A group of children scampered down to the river bank, calling out to Drew excitedly. He leapt out of the canoe and pulled it up on to a small shingle bank similar to the one by the waterfall, and immediately the children clustered round him, laughing, and clutching at his hand, welcoming him as a familiar friend.

Briar viewed the scene with undisguised astonishment. One moment they were being hooked along the dark tunnel of the river, and the next, without any warning, the claustrophobic greenery vanished into a wide clearing, which held an enormous wooden dwelling, raised high on stilts similar to the *pondoks*, but this building, she judged, must be well over a hundred feet in length.

Longhouse was an apt description. Unlike the *pondoks*, which were used merely as temporary shelters until it was time for the construction crew to move on again, this was a venerable structure, built for permanent use—the jungle's answer to a row of semis.

Her interested gaze noticed doors, ensuring the privacy of each small family unit, and the wide communal veranda that stretched the whole length of the dwelling, where those families could gather for company whenever they wished. In spite of the size of the longhouse, however, the place appeared to be deserted, apart from the children.

'Where is everybody?' she asked, and dropped Drew's helping hand with nervous haste the moment her feet touched terra firma.

'At this time of the day everybody's away working in the fields, further up the mountain. Only the very old, and the very young, and the sick, are left in the village until the others return in the evening.'

Exactly the same as commuters at home, Briar thought, and smiled at the children who clustered round Drew. They looked the picture of health. They stared back at her with a mixture of curiosity and shyness, and she exclaimed regretfully, 'I wish I'd brought my camera along with me!'

'You wouldn't have been able to use it, if you had.'

'It's got a built-in flash. It would have coped with the poor light.'

The children's pale, creamy skin, which in the perpetual twilight of their forest home did not need any darker pigment to protect it from the fierce rays of the Equatorial sun, added to their shining dark eyes and straight black hair, was an irresistible attraction to any camera enthusiast.

'They don't like their image being taken by a stranger. They fear it will put them in that stranger's power.'

Briar nodded, suddenly sober. She shared the children's fear, but for a different reason, reinforced as she watched Drew's easy magnetism exert itself on the small group. She already knew from his attitude towards Tim that he liked children, and the response of the little ones crowded about him now, completely unafraid, told her that they did not need to be related to like him in return.

He distributed the expected sweets, then bent and clapped his hands mock-fiercely behind them, and they scampered away towards the longhouse, squealing in pretended fright, and ran laughing up the notched pole to the veranda, with a nonchalance that made Briar catch her breath with fear for the safety of the smallest ones, some scarcely more than toddlers.

She need not have worried. They all reached the veranda without mishap, and ran along it, calling out to someone whom Briar could not see from the ground. Drew put one foot on the pole to follow them, then paused.

'Do you need any help?' he asked.

'No, thanks,' Briar refused quickly. 'I've got the knack by now.'

She hoped fervently that it was not an empty boast. The longhouse stilts were several feet higher than those of the *pondoks*, and the angle of the pole was that much more alarming. Keeping her fingers surreptitiously crossed, she resisted the urge to go down on all fours, and drove her feet to follow Drew, while she remained precariously upright.

'So you have,' he mocked when she stepped on to the safety of the veranda, and his look laughed at the fingers which she had forgotten to uncross, but, before she had a chance to retort, he turned to a wizened old man who squatted against the rails at the other end of the long structure.

'Balang!' the senior greeted the engineer.

The old man was heavily tattooed, like Lan, and Briar's startled look took in ear-lobes which were

distended to shoulder-length by heavy brass ear-
rings. Even as she watched, the man turned and
directed a stream of bright red saliva through the
veranda rails on to the ground below, and she saw
that his mouth and gums were stained the fiery
colour of the habitual betel nut chewer, but his
manner was regal as he greeted Drew, and his
words, spoken in passable English, gave her another
shock.

'You have brought your woman,' he observed.

'I'm——' Briar exploded, but her, 'no such
thing,' gagged to a halt on Drew's thunderous glare.
It said Be quiet! as clearly as if he had shouted the
words aloud.

'She is honoured to visit you,' he answered their
host, and Briar gritted her teeth in a fierce effort
to prevent her indignant denial from emerging.

Drew appeared to be completely at home in this
strange world of half-light and exotic plants and
people. She was the outsider, and reason told her
that she must defer to his superior knowledge of
the local culture, no matter how much it rasped her
pride to do so, but her unuttered disclaimer stuck
like an indigestible lump in her throat, which made
the drink brought by a young girl who appeared
from behind one of the rattan doors all the more
welcome.

The girl was young and lissome and lovely, and
she moved with the unconscious grace of her
people. Was she the one for whom Drew had
bought the sarong? Briar put the question away
from her, just as she had tried to put away the image
of the girl in the college punt, but they joined forces
in the back of her mind, and in spite of her efforts

insisted on remaining there, two questions to which she could not decide whether she wanted to know the answers or not.

Drew lowered himself easily to the floor and sat cross-legged, facing the old man, his relaxed posture suggesting that he had sat this way many times before, After a moment's hesitation Briar did likewise, sitting close to his side.

The young girl spread a length of cloth on the floor between Drew and the old man, and set on it a tall pottery jar, which Briar saw contained a clear liquid. Three drinking vessels were placed beside the jar, their patterns matching the larger container.

Briar regarded the ceramics with interest. She did not need to be an expert in antiques to see that they were very old, and in a wonderful state of preservation. Their Chinese origin was immediately obvious from the nature of the decoration, and the peculiarly lovely glaze. Rich pickings, indeed, for a gang of unscrupulous raiders.

Drew turned and spoke to the girl, saying something in her own language. She smiled at him, a bewitching curling of her lips that irradiated her face and made her dark eyes sparkle. Immediately she bent to retrieve one of the drinking vessels, at the same time casting a merry look at Briar, making the latter suspect that she must be the subject of Drew's remark, and that it had not been to her advantage.

Her ire rose as the girl disappeared with the vessel behind one of the rattan doors, then reappeared with a platter of fruit in its place, which she set significantly in front of Briar.

The message was clear: the drink was for the men, and she, Briar, was expected to confine her attentions to the fruit. She felt like a six-year-old being offered a toffee to pacify her, while the grown-ups drank wine. It was Drew's fault. He had deliberately denied her. He must have told the girl to take away the drinking vessel, in order to remove temptation from her reach, but what explanation he offered for his request Briar did not like to conjecture.

Her thirst increased, along with her vexation. The steamy heat of her surroundings drew perspiration in rivulets down her face, and parched her throat, and she longed to tip up the jar and fill her dry mouth with whatever liquid it contained.

She thrust at Drew, *sotto voce*, 'I need a drink as well as you!'

'The melon will quench your thirst.'

He pulled a knife from his pocket, **and**, picking up the fruit, sliced it neatly, scooped out the seeds, then fitted the pieces back together again and placed it in front of Briar, for her to help herself. She regarded the dissected yellow globe with disfavour.

'I need a *real* drink,' she persisted.

'You can't drink *arak*. It's rice wine, and it's got a kick like a mule. It's definitely not for the uninitiated.'

The old man decided the argument. How much of it he understood, Briar could not tell, and the copious tattooing on his face effectively masked its expression as he reached forward to pick up the jar and filled the two drinking cups to the brim. He handed one to Drew, and took the other himself, then started to talk in his own language, which Briar was unable to follow, but it was plain that Drew understood every word.

She sank her teeth into a slice of the melon. The juicy flesh quenched her thirst, but it did nothing to take away her irritation.

Shortly afterwards Drew rose to his feet and announced, 'I'm going to the end room of the longhouse. You stay here—I may be some time.'

Her sarcastic, 'Yes, my lord,' was not totally muffled by the melon.

His look told her that his quick ears had registered her shot, and his jaw tightened, but he made no reply as he pivoted on his heel and disappeared behind a distant rattan door.

To join the girl who had served him with the drink?

Briar nearly choked on a piece of melon. Recovering herself with a gulp, she left the rest of the fruit untouched, her mouth gone unaccountably dry again, but her appetite for the fruit vanished.

Drew was gone for a long time. At first the old man filled it with talk, all of it about Drew.

'Balang is a good man,' the old voice intoned.

'Why do you call him Balang? What does it mean?' asked Briar, in a not very successful attempt to prevent her mind from following the subject of their conversation through the now closed door.

'We call him Tiger because he is strong and fearless. Since he came, the robbers have left us alone. When our young people are away in the fields we feel safe, because Balang is here. He is stronger than the robbers. Stronger, even, than the jungle itself. The legends of my people say that such a man is suckled on tiger's milk, to make him stronger than other men.'

His head nodded, and he dozed, made sleepy by the weight of his years and the strength of the rice wine. Briar wondered if it might be having the same effect on Drew. She sat on, growing increasingly restless. Her watch told her that nearly an hour had passed since Drew had left. The unevenness of the rough-hewn wooden planks underneath her dug in through the thin cotton of her trousers, and she wriggled impatiently. It was too bad of him to keep her hanging about like this. She flapped her hand irritably at a persistent fly. Whatever Drew was doing, or whoever he was with, she decided to go and see for herself.

The end room, he had said. Briar stood in front of the rattan door and hesitated, recalling Drew's angry reaction when she had followed him to the airstrip.

If he was with the girl, he would be even angrier. She hesitated no longer. Raising her hand, she gave the door an unnecessarily hard push. Tiger or not, Drew could not eat her, for coming in search of him.

A heavy, foetid smell hit her nostrils the moment she stepped inside. She gagged, and raised a hand to her mouth and nose to cut it off, and Drew turned sharply from where he knelt beside something on the other side of the small room. At the sight of her, a black scowl crossed his forehead.

'I told you to stay where you were!'

'I got tired of waiting for you to come back.'

Would the girl in the punt, in faraway England, get tired of waiting for him too? Or would she con-

sider any length of wait worthwhile if Drew came
back to her at the end of it?

Briar narrowed her eyes, adjusting them to the
dim light, curious to see what Drew was doing.
Patches of white revealed themselves as packets of
sterile dressings, such as she had used on his own
head. Something squirmed and gave a thin wail
from the floor beside him, and what had appeared
at first sight to be just a bundle on a mat revealed
itself as a small child.

Briar's heart contracted. The weak cry brought
memories crowding back, and for a dreadful
moment a blackness threatened to overwhelm her.
The child cried again, and with a strength of will
she did not know she possessed, Briar forced herself
to look at it.

The baby was older than Lucy, perhaps one or
two years old. It was difficult to tell, it looked so
ill. Suppurating sores disfigured the small body and
gave her the reason for the awful smell, and,
sickened by the sight, Briar hurriedly turned her
eyes away, and on to the face of a woman who was
crouched on the floor nearby.

What she read there shocked her almost as much
as the condition of the baby. In the dull eyes and
the drooping lips was a helpless, hopeless resig-
nation, that accepted the fact that her child was
going to die.

A shaft of unbearable pain made Briar gasp out
loud. She herself had endured the same un-
speakable agony, the same helpless despair. But this
woman's child was still alive. Perhaps by some
miracle . . .

'Come outside,' Drew ordered her curtly, and rose to his feet.

'Finish what you were doing.' She should not have interrupted him. She would not have done so, if he had only explained.

'I've done all I can for now.' With a low word to the woman, Drew grasped Briar by the arm and propelled her forcefully outside, but instead of going back along the veranda to join the old man, he led her down another notched pole and along a wide jungle trail, away from the village and the longhouse, to where a persistent roar announced another waterfall. Here he stopped by some rocks out of reach of the spray, and ordered her briefly to, 'Sit down.'

In spite of her shaking legs, Briar refused. 'I'll stand,' she told him. From Drew's tone, she sensed battle, and she did not want to reduce her already diminutive height, and so give him the greater advantage. He lost no time in firing the opening shot.

'Why didn't you do as I told you to, and stay on the veranda until I came back?'

'Why should I? Contrary to popular belief, I am *not* your woman!' The old man's categorisation still stung, and she allowed her resentment to surface.

'If you were, I'd have taught you better sense.'

'Like how?' flashed Briar, and stopped aghast as his eyes fired.

'Like this,' he grated.

Too late, she saw the folly of teasing a tiger. His arms pinioned her. His lips devoured her. And the sense which he'd threatened to teach her wavered helplessly beneath the onslaught of his kiss. Desperately Briar strained away from him, but his strength laughed at her puny defences, and in despair she felt her body begin to go pliant in his arms. A tiny moan broke from her imprisoned lips. If he held her like this for much longer, she would be lost.

Like a drowning swimmer clutching at a straw, she clung on to the promise of the helicopter, perhaps due to arrive tomorrow morning. When she escaped from the jungle, and from Drew, the senses that were drowning now would surface and struggle to the shore, there to remain safely out of reach of twin grey pools, darkened to fathomless depths by a passion that woke a traitorous echo in herself.

When Drew released her, Briar's trembling legs deposited her willy-nilly on to the rock on which he had ordered her to sit in the first place. He growled,

'Let that be a reminder not to take chances! For all you knew, the child might have been suffering from a highly infectious disease.'

Her throbbing lips would need no reminder. Briar felt as if they would carry the imprint of Drew's kiss, like a brand mark, for the rest of her days. Almost too numb to form words, they muttered in her defence,

'I didn't know the child was in there.'

She had suspected it was the young girl instead. With ruthless self-honesty, she knew she had gone through the rattan door, hoping that it was not, and, contrarily, hoping that it was. If it had been, and the girl and Drew had been making love, it would have stripped away his magnetism and left her, Briar, free.

It had not been the girl, and her hammering heart warned her how easily she might become a captive. Hastily she shored up her defences with a question.

'Is the baby...has it got...?' Her voice trailed to a halt. The possibility of being exposed to an infectious disease had simply not occurred to her. As so many other things had not occurred to her, until too late, and the possible consequences made a mounting total that, if she was not very careful, might cost her dear.

'Fortunately the boy isn't infectious. But it would have been all the same if he was. As an outsider, you've got no natural immunity. You're a sitting target to any ill-disposed bug on the loose.'

'What's wrong with the baby?'

'He met up with a caterpillar.'

Briar bridled. 'There's no need to be sarcastic!'

'I'm not. It's the truth. There's one particular species of caterpillar in this part of the world that releases its hairs when it feels threatened. They dig into whatever they touch, and burrow right down under the skin, and the wounds turn septic. They're the reason for the sores on the child's body. They're also another reason why you mustn't wander about on your own. You don't know what might be lethal and what's not.'

Tigers were just about as lethal as you could get, Briar brooded, and the one standing in front of her surpassed all. Out loud she said,

'There must be something we can do for him.'

She was unconscious of the 'we', and of the quick flicker of Drew's eyes that registered what her own stunned mind did not.

'He can't be moved against his parents' will.'

'We can't just leave the child here to die!' Oh, Lucy, Lucy! You had all the care that love could give you, but it didn't save you. Briar forced out through a closing throat, 'He needs hospital attention. Up here in a jungle hut, he doesn't stand a chance.'

'I know that. It's only the penicillin I've been dressing his sores with that's kept him going until now. How much longer it will hold his condition stable, I wouldn't like to guess.'

'Then *do* something, Drew.' Impelled by unbearable memories, Briar jumped to her feet and grasped his arms with both her hands, and shook him, as if by sheer force she could make him accomplish the impossible. 'You can't just abandon the child to his fate, as his mother seems to have done. She hasn't even bothered to brush the room. All those withered leaves and twigs...'

Her voice cracked, and she was too shocked to resist when Drew reached out and pulled her to him, but gently this time, all his anger gone. Hastily, Briar turned her face away, to hide a humiliating trickle down her cheek, and stiffened as she felt something pass lightly over the top of her curls.

Its touch was like the breath of a breeze, but none stirred the surrounding forest greenery. Her heart began to pound with slow, painful strokes, and she did not know whether to blame her distress on seeing the baby's condition, or Drew's closeness, or a mixture of both, for trying her self-control to the limit.

Drew's voice rumbled deep in his chest. 'The boy's mother *is* doing something, according to her. Those withered leaves and twigs are spirit offerings for the baby's recovery.' His expression was grave, respecting the mother's belief, and it cut off Briar's scornful ejaculation and replaced it with a strained,

'It isn't enough. Surely she can see that?'

'I know. She's beginning to know it too. I've tried each day, for the last three days, to persuade her to accept hospital treatment for the baby, but each time she's refused. Today she went so far as to say that if the child is no better by this evening she'll think about it.'

The mother of the baby would surely not leave the longhouse, and her sick child, to go to the landing strip to see Drew. Which meant that, for four days, he had made the arduous journey up-river to the village to see her.

Would go again that same evening, poling the dugout canoe against the torrential current on each repeated trip, any one of which was sufficient to sap a giant's energy, but did not deter this man, whom they called Tiger, from spending his own strength in order to help a sick baby.

Back at the construction camp that evening, when the work was over for the day, Drew made preparations for his return trip to the longhouse, searching out fresh medical equipment from his store to take with him.

'You'll be exhausted!' Briar protested. 'Can't you leave it until the morning?'

'The helicopter will be here in the morning, with spares for Lan's tractor. If I can manage to persuade the mother to bring the baby with me tonight, we can airlift them to hospital tomorrow, with no more delay. Another twenty-four hours might tip the balance. I daren't take a chance on the baby's life by leaving the trip until daylight. You'll be safe enough here. Lan will be with you until I return.'

It was not her own safety which concerned Briar, but Drew's. The dangers of the trip up-river in the daylight were bad enough. Darkness would multiply them a thousand times, added to which there was the possibility that the raiders might sneak back, to wreak vengeance for their painful lesson of the night before. If they caught Drew on his own, even a tiger must be helpless to combat such overwhelming odds.

She begged impulsively, 'Let me come with you. I may be able to help with the baby,' she excused her offer.

Drew looked at her for a long moment before he answered slowly, 'You'll have to stay here. There's only room in the canoe for two.'

If there had been room for more, would he have let her go along with him? It was pointless to ask, since there could be no answer, but as the hours ticked by, and still the engineer did not return, Briar grew more and more uneasy.

'I keep wondering if the mother will agree to let Drew bring her baby back,' she excused her restlessness to Lan, who had come to sit with her on the veranda of the *pondok*. It was easy enough to voice her thoughts to Lan. Why was it not equally simple to bare her heart to Drew? There was no answer to that either.

Lan said calmly, 'Drew will do all he can to persuade the mother.'

'I wish I knew. The baby was so dreadfully ill,' sighed Briar. Memory of the sick child haunted her, a small, wailing helplessness to add to the ghost of Lucy.

'You'll know when Drew gets back. If he has the mother and child with him, he'll have succeeded. If he's alone, he'll have failed,' Lan said, with the fatalism which seemed so much a part of jungle philosophy, and which Briar's western outlook found so difficult to accept.

Failure and Drew did not go together, she tried to boost her spirits, while her eyes strained on the spot where the track to the river led into the undergrowth, willing Drew to appear.

Why doesn't he come? she cried silently for the hundredth time. Had the child's mother refused to accept the help he offered? Had the baby died in the meantime? It was not impossible.

Had Drew himself met with an accident? That was not impossible either, in spite of his amazing strength. The hazards of poling up-river were many, and daunting. Underwater snags, avoidable by day, would be invisible in the darkness, and even a man as strong as Drew must sometimes bow to Nature's superior strength.

'Don't sit there daydreaming, Briar. Come and lend a hand.'

It was Drew. He was safe! He strode, tall and commanding, out of the jungle, and across the clearing towards the *pondok*, calling to her peremptorily as he came, ordering, not asking her, to come and help him.

But—he was safe!

Briar flew to meet him, relief carrying her down the notched pole with a reckless disregard for broken ankles. She saw without surprise that he had

the woman and baby with him. She had not
seriously expected him to fail. Drew himself would
not expect to fail. He was so confident, so supremely sure of his own ability to rise victorious
over every situation.

He carried the evidence of his victory in his arms.
Fresh dressings, and bandages starkly white, to
match the one on his own forehead, bound the
child's small body, and the mother followed a meek
few paces behind him. At any other time such sub-
servience would have irritated Briar, but in the relief
at seeing them safe it passed her by. Drew was not
alone in his love for children.

'How is he?' she demanded urgently, by way of
a greeting, and Drew shot her a probing look, but,
impatient for his answer, she disregarded it. 'Tell
me!'

'With a bit of luck, we may be in time. Help me
to make up a bed for the baby. They'll stay in our
pondok until the helicopter comes tomorrow.'

Our pondok... A strange thrill ran through Briar
as she fled to do Drew's bidding. The small, limp
form cradled in his arms acted as a spur that made
her ruthless in her choice of Drew's sleeping mat,
and the soft blanket which the engineer had given
her for her own use, to ward off the chill of the
night mists.

He bent and laid the child down gently on to the
hastily assembled bed, and the mother crept to the
baby's head and resumed her position there as if
she were still in her longhouse home. Drew
straightened, and for the first time Briar noticed
the lines of tiredness that not even his iron self-
control could completely erase from his face.

He said, 'They need food,' and she responded quickly, 'So do you. Stay here—I'll get it. You look shattered.'

A strange expression flitted for a moment across his face, but Briar was already on her way to the crew's cooking fires, and did not see. She returned a few minutes later, laden with food which the crew had kept hot for the travellers from their own evening meal. Bowls of thick stew and plates of rice for Drew and the woman, and a bowl of soup for the baby, which Lan told her contained herbs which should help reduce the child's fever.

'Sit down and eat your own meal. I'll feed the baby,' Briar pressed her offerings into the hands of the adults, reassuring Drew when he hesitated, 'I'm quite capable of looking after a sick baby.'

She had had enough experience, goodness knew, and the pain of it returned to torment her as she spooned liquid, drop by drop, into the small fever-parched mouth, but bravely she ignored it, conscious of the similar battle which had been lost with such devastating consequences to herself, and this time simply must be won, in order to save another woman from the same suffering.

The chill river mist rose, to make ghosts of the trees, and with it the child's fever increased, and as soon as he had eaten Drew took turns with Briar to tend their restless patient.

Gradually the furtive sounds of the jungle gave way to the patter of the night rain, the mist thickened and enveloped the *pondok*, and there was only herself and Drew, isolated in the soft pool of lamplight shed by the storm lantern which he had placed on the table on his side of the veranda. To

give them more room, he had tied up the rattan
screen to the roof beam.

Soothed by Lan's brew, the baby eventually
dropped off into an exhausted sleep, and Briar sat
back on her heels and passed a weary hand over
her forehead.

Drew gruffed, 'Get some rest. You can use my
sleeping blanket.'

'No, you need rest more than I do. I'll stick it
out with you.'

Weary though she was, Briar was hurting too
much to rest. Memories crowded in on her, each
one bringing its own pain, and she had long since
discovered that it was better to work than to weep.
She draped Drew's blanket instead across the
shoulders of the child's mother, and received in
return a soft-eyed look of gratitude that tran-
scended the language barrier, as, enveloped in its
cosy warmth, the older woman slept too, and left
Briar and Drew alone to watch.

Tiredness and strain eroded daytime barriers.
Crouched on the rough-hewn planks, a mere foot
away from where Drew sat facing her on the child's
other side, Briar had no defence against her own
essential femininity.

The baby murmured and tossed in its sleep, and
they both reached out simultaneously to tuck the
blanket round him again. Their hands met and
touched on the fold of cloth, and sharp sensation
shot through Briar's arms, as if a tiger's claw had
dug into her fingers.

Drew said abruptly, 'I'll brew some coffee. It'll
help to keep us both awake,' and Briar nodded
without speaking. She did not need coffee to help

her. Her body was tired, but her turbulent mind had never felt further from sleep.

Stripped of daylight's false identities, they were returned to their roots in the darkness, and they became man and woman, each one rawly aware of the other, neither speaking, but each feeling, and knowing that the other felt too.

The sputter and hiss of the small camp Primus stove, and the faint smell of paraffin, seemed to come from another world, a safe, sane world, where elemental things could be disregarded, as the brooding presence of the jungle night refused to allow itself to be disregarded, pressing in on them like a tangible threat.

Briar took her mug of coffee from Drew's hand with fingers that shook. The brew was strong, and laced with the sickly sweetness of condensed milk, designed to act as a booster to throbbing nerves that needed no such stimulation. She wished raggedly that drowsiness *would* get the upper hand, and so release her from this total awareness of Drew, that, however much she fought against it, was there, and could not be denied.

The woman she was reached out to the man he was, and fear lay starkly in between. A detached part of Briar's mind watched the byplay as if it were being enacted on a stage, set apart, a silent mime that was yet loud with unspoken words.

It saw the coffee slop to the rim of her mug, betraying the uncontrollable shaking of her fingers. It noticed Drew's swift glance register this evidence of her nerves, and caught the quick fire that burned in his eyes, triumphant, because he knew that he was the cause.

CHAPTER EIGHT

BRIAR watched the helicopter manoeuvre to land, with the same desperate anticipation with which the captain of a sinking ship must watch the approach of a lifeboat.

Had it come in time?

She swept aside Lan's thoughtful, 'Ranjit may not be able to take you all. It will depend upon what sort of load he's carrying already.'

'He's *got* to take me! I can't stay here any longer.'

Overwrought by the tensions of the night, Briar was careless about letting her need for deliverance show. 'He *must* take me,' she insisted.

Drew drawled, 'Have you hated being in the jungle so much?'

'Do you expect me to *like* a place that harbours bandits and poisonous caterpillars?' Briar flashed.

And tigers, she made the silent addition.

'You should have stayed in Singapore.'

If he tells me that again, I'll scream! Briar promised herself. Keeping a tight rein on her self-control, she said, 'When I came, I expected to be here for only a few hours. Whatever you might believe, I really did think Ranjit would be coming back to collect me the same day.'

If only he had!

If only she had been able to remain for a few hours, and then go back to Singapore, and from there home to Tony, with her contract to Drew finished, she would still be in control of herself, and her destiny. She would not now be threatened with a repeat of that trauma which she had only just managed to put behind her, and now, because of Drew, she felt the control slipping from her grasp, and she feared the consequences more now than she had before.

Then, emotionally, she had been an inexperienced girl. The break-up with Philip had turned her into a woman, but the woman she had become had discovered, to her dismay, that emotional maturity was not an insurance against heartache.

She must get away, now, before the heartache became heartbreak.

She could not return to work with Tony. Bitterly she acknowledged that Drew had denied her that avenue of escape. In the small county town it was inevitable that she and he would meet, and not knowing when or where would be a constant strain on nerves which were already stretched to breaking point, and that she was not prepared to endure.

It would be far safer to return to the clinic, and her old job there. In London, she would have less chance of meeting with Philip than she had of bumping into Drew in Warwick, and of the two she acknowledged that the latter prospect held the most terrors for her.

Briar sighed. Was unhappiness to pursue her for the rest of her life? Was she doomed to always flee, just one step ahead of love?

'When Ranjit brought me here, I didn't expect to stay one night, let alone two,' she insisted.

'That must have put you in quite a spot.' The young Indian pilot ran surefootedly up the notched pole, and gained the veranda of the *pondok* in time to hear Briar's remark. 'I should have told you,' he apologised, 'but when you said you were Drew's personal assistant I assumed you'd know all about the timing of the regular flights across the islands.'

Carefully Briar kept her eyes averted from Drew's face. At least he knew, now, that she had not described herself as his wife or his girlfriend. The knowledge gave her scant satisfaction when the pilot confirmed Lan's suspicion.

'I shan't be able to ferry you out until tomorrow, I'm afraid.'

'I can't stay here any longer!' Briar's voice rose, and the pilot looked his consternation at Drew.

'I can't take more than one with me—I've got a load of equipment on board, to return to base. There isn't room for more than one adult in the cabin.'

'Surely you can squeeze the two of us in? We're neither of us very big.'

Drew intervened, and his voice was stern, 'If Ranjit says he can only take one, he means just that. He's limited by his payload. It has to be you or the mother and her baby. It's a straight choice.'

Cruelly, he left the choice to Briar. Ranjit consoled, 'I'll be back here first thing tomorrow morning. It will only mean waiting for another twenty-four hours.'

Another twenty-four hours might be too late, both for herself and for the baby. The choice was no choice at all. Feeling as if she was purchasing the baby's future with her own, Briar forced out, 'You must take the mother and her baby.'

'The message is getting through,' jibed Drew, so low that only Briar could hear, and she pulled in a difficult breath.

Other messages were getting through, none of them welcome, especially the one that gloated, Drew has won—again.

She must not allow him to win the final battle, to lay siege to her heart. If that vital organ was taken from her keeping for a second time, it would surely cease to beat.

With a feeling of numb fatality, she helped the mother to board the helicopter, carrying her sick baby. She even managed an encouraging smile as the cabin door closed behind the two, and Drew pulled her back to stand beside him, out of the way of the mini dust storm which was sucked up by the whirling rotor-blades, as Ranjit took his craft up, to hover for a moment above the clearing before it disappeared over the rim of the trees.

Briar's eyes were bleak as she stood staring after it. Another twenty-four hours... She nerved herself to face them. Tonight she would plead tiredness, she planned, and turn in early, immediately after the evening meal was over. That way she would escape that dangerously intimate time with Drew, alone on the lamplit veranda of the *pondok*.

The hours of daylight that stood between then and now posed quite a different problem. How to fill them? She had to find an occupation to stop herself from thinking.

Drew provided her with an unexpected answer, that was no answer at all to her problem.

'The jungle isn't all bad,' he told her gravely. 'After you've put a fresh dressing on my head, I'll take you and show you the other side of it—the beautiful side. Then you won't leave with the wrong impression.'

The strongest impressions she would take away with her would not be of the jungle itself, Briar thought. Other impressions superimposed themselves, like dressing the wound on Drew's forehead. In the bustle of getting the mother and baby into the helicopter, she had forgotten this other necessary task. She backed away from it now with a hasty, 'You'll be able to put it on yourself this morning.'

'If I do, I won't be able to see if the cut's healing properly. We don't run to mirrors in the camp, and I mustn't bother Lan to look after me. He's busy attending to the line-up of his own walking wounded.'

Which only left Briar. She dared not refuse, in case the wound should show signs of turning septic, and need more urgent attention. Drew's earlier warning about this very danger drove her into a corner from which there was no escape.

'Wash the dust off your face, then, while I look out a clean dressing to put on,' she told him, and scorned the quaver which she could not erase from her voice, that had been meant to sound brisk and professional and disinterested, and failed lamentably.

Drew's look questioned the quaver, but he made no comment, and a couple of minutes later, soaped and swilled and towelled, he presented her with the task from which she shrank.

The edges of the wound were already knitting together cleanly, with the aid of a superbly fit body, but swabbing and re-dressing it stretched Briar's self-control to the limit. In self-defence she stood behind Drew to perform her task, where he could not look into her face, and in a moment realised her mistake when he leaned his head back against her instead, the better to allow her to reach the cut on his forehead.

The pressure of his dark head resting against her caused her heart to race, and after she applied the new sterilised dressing, and taped it securely in place with fingers made clumsy by nerves, the feel of it remained with Briar, a heavy weight in the present, and, if she was not careful, a burden to carry with her into the future.

Lan came with them on their excursion into the jungle.

The presence of Drew's tattooed opposite number distanced Briar from the engineer, and took away the knife-edge of uncertainty. It set her free to enjoy to the full the clouds of butterflies which settled in mass brilliance on a sunny mud bank of a forest pool, and her breathless, 'Oh, how lovely!' drew smiles from the men when the insects suddenly rose into the air and filled the forest clearing with a fluttering rainbow.

Lan guided them to a spot where orchids grew, low down on the mossy trunks of trees. 'Most of them grow on the very top of the forest canopy, to get the light, so you aren't able to see them,' he explained, but these grew in abundance, near to the ground.

Drew plucked one, and, after examining it to make sure that no insects lurked in its vivid depths, he tucked it in Briar's curls, teasing, 'An orchid for my lady.'

She was not his lady. She would never be any man's lady, ever again. But, because Lan was with them, she was able to laugh, and the moment passed without too much embarrassment.

Briar was awed into silence by the sight of a waterfall, which rivalled Niagara in height, and when she found her voice it was to mourn, 'All this beauty, and at the rate they're cutting down the rain forests it will soon be gone for ever.'

'Public demand might save the forests yet,' Drew comforted.

'Isn't it public demand for the timber which is destroying them?'

'At the moment,' Drew agreed. 'But people's perception is changing. They're becoming aware of the consequences of their actions, and the publicity is making them want to come and see these places for themselves, not just view them on a television screen. The turnaround has happened already, with wild life. People used to go on safari with guns. Now they take cameras to shoot instead. The same thing could happen with the forests. Tourism might preserve them, where nothing else can.'

'If tourists come, the forests won't remain unspoiled as they are now. There'll be a price to pay.'

There was always a price to pay for everything, Briar reflected wearily. Most times, the cost was not worth the commodity, and the instalments carried on for far too long. Hastily she thrust the errant thought away from her. Today was too good to spoil with past regrets.

'There's always a price to pay,' Drew echoed her thoughts. 'But it will be worth it if it buys the life of the forests. At least tourism can be controlled.'

Would she be able to control the future loneliness of an empty heart? Briar wondered. The thought pursued her. She could fill her days with work. But what of the nights? it persisted. What of the nights?

The night ahead of her must be endured first, and to Briar's relief Lan elected to remain with them on their return to camp. He shared their evening meal, and stayed on afterwards to talk shop with Drew.

'Ranjit will be here with the rest of the spares in the morning, and then we'll be operational again.' He turned to Briar with a smile. 'You'll soon be on your way home, and Drew will follow you. I shall miss you both.'

How soon would Drew follow her? Briar tensed, then relaxed as the engineer remarked, 'I should be clear of this trip in another three or four days. Unless an emergency crops up, I won't need to come out again until this airstrip is ready to be commissioned, and the next one started.'

Three or four days. That would give her ample time to check out from the hotel, perhaps do a little shopping, and still be away before Drew got back to Singapore, Briar calculated. And, too, it meant that she would be well ahead of Drew in returning to England.

She would go back to Warwick, and tell Tony that, now she had time to think things over, she had decided to return to her old job right away, after all. That way she could lose herself in the anonymous crowds of the capital, before Drew returned to the Paddocks and discovered she was gone.

'I think I'll pack my things before I turn in.' Drew rose from his chair and stretched himself lazily. 'If they're done, I shan't need to keep Ranjit waiting if he's early coming for us in the morning.'

'*Us?*' Briar gulped.

The word forced itself from between clenched teeth. It could not happen twice! To be on the very verge of escape, and then to be dragged back once again to endure another—how many hours?—in Drew's company, before she could be free, was unthinkable. But it was happening.

She supposed it was silly of her to assume that Drew's further three or four days would all be spent with Lan and his team, on site. Just how silly, his next words confirmed.

'I'm coming back to Singapore with you. I've finished all I can do here. There are just a few loose ends to be tied up with the various interested parties in the city, and then I shall follow you home.'

Not come with her. That would be too much.

But, no matter how quickly Ranjit returned them to Singapore, Briar knew she could not hope to obtain a flight home the same day. It would be at least a further twenty-four hours before she would be able to get a booking, which took up two days of Drew's possible three or four. If he only remained for three, that left her with a margin of only one day in which to manoeuvre.

Surely not even her evil luck could fill all the vacant seats on the London-bound air-liners, until it was time for Drew to return as well? If she absolutely had to, she could manage to cope with one more day in his company. But no more. *Please*, no more, her weary senses sent up a silent prayer, as, with the rattan curtain firmly pulled down between them, she felt into a troubled sleep that made her last night in the jungle as restless as her first.

She gained some small comfort from Ranjit's greeting the next morning. He announced cheerfully, 'There's a meeting scheduled for the moment you land, Drew. I've arranged for a car to take Briar straight to the hotel. It will come back for you later, when the meeting's finished.

Briar's spirits rose. Most of Drew's previous meetings had carried on until very late in the evening. She would go to bed early, before he returned to the hotel, and with any luck she would be on her way to the airport the next morning, while he was engaged in yet more discussions.

Drew shot down her hastily formed plan with the command, 'Don't book dinner for yourself at the hotel, Briar. We'll go somewhere special for your last night in Singapore.'

'But your meeting...' she protested. A tête-à-tête dinner with Drew was the last thing she felt capable of coping with.

'The first meeting won't take long. It's only a site progress report, to bring up anything which needs to be added to the agendas of the main meetings afterwards.'

There was to be no escape.

With a feeling of inevitability, Briar prepared for dinner that evening. 'Be ready by seven o'clock,' Drew told her. It was six o'clock now. There was time to relax for a little while longer, if relax was the right word. All the butterflies she had encountered in the forest clearing seemed to take flight in Briar's stomach, making the prospect of food an added ordeal.

Her eyes stared back at her from the dressing-table mirror. They were wider than usual, and their pupils several shades darker, indicative of stress, but Briar congratulated herself that this was the only visible sign of her inner turbulence. Outwardly she remained calm enough, poised, cool even, and she hoped fervently that she would have the strength to remain so for the rest of the evening.

Her dress was one she had worn before, with the embroidered roses round the hem. She pulled the belt tight, and reached into the drawer for a handkerchief to tuck in her bracelet. A quick search told her that the laundry had not yet returned her favourite, the one bearing the embroidered rose to complement her dress. Perhaps they had lost it. She shrugged. It was a small setback, not to be compared to the difficulties presented by the rest of the evening. She selected another lace-edged square— then froze with it in her hand as a voice reached her ears from the sitting-room outside.

Drew's voice. The sound of it vibrated her taut nerves, and threatened her fragile composure. A quick hiss of relief escaped her as other voices joined in. Drew spoke again, a man answered him, to be echoed by a woman's soft laugh. Had Elizabeth and Robert returned? If so, they could not have done so at a more opportune moment.

'Briar? Briar, are you there?' Drew called, and relief made Briar's voice almost gay as she called back,

'Coming!'

Deliverance had arrived out of the blue, just as it had with Lan yesterday. Having the company of other people meant that she would be able to abandon her defences and enjoy her last night in Singapore too. Perhaps then the memories she would carry away with her, added to those other lovely memories of her last day in the jungle, would in time help to erase the darker side of her stay, and eventually allow her some peace.

'Come and meet Grant and Ella,' Drew invited. Not Elizabeth and Robert, but no matter. Anybody would do, so long as she did not have to be alone with Drew.

'We're all working together on the project,' he explained. 'Grant and Ella are both medics. They're doing part fieldwork, and part plant research.'

In spite of their obvious commitment to their work, the pair did not allow it to intrude upon their evening off. With typical American exuberance, they made the most of their free time, and tempted Briar to throw caution to the winds and herself soak up every moment of the spectacular dinner cruise round the harbour, the 'something special' which more than lived up to Drew's promise.

Talk at the dinner table ranged from bowling to Beethoven, and only once, from Briar's point of view, did the conversation verge on the dangerous. Ella confided, 'As soon as the airstrips are finished, and we've got the whole thing working, Grant and I are hoping to set up a permanent home and start a family. It will mean waiting for another twelve months or so, because as we are now we're constantly moving from place to place, and I think it's important for children to have a settled home background.' Taking Briar's agreement for granted, she chatted on happily.

'I plan to give up work while the children are little, of course. We'd like four. How many do you reckon on having, Briar? Eventually, I mean?' Her laughing glance took in Briar's ringless left hand.

Briar tensed, and unconsciously her fingers stole upwards to caress the precious keepsake, safe inside her locket.

'I hadn't given numbers much thought,' she managed, and was surprised to hear how controlled her voice sounded, coming from a throat that felt tight with sudden tears.

'I think it's important for a mother to be around while the children are small, don't you?' Ella persisted, and Briar thought, She doesn't intend to be a weekend wife. She would suit Drew.

She could feel the engineer's eyes home in on her face, watching for its ever revealing expression, waiting for her reply. The silence stretched, and became loaded. It was as if Grant and Ella were not there. Only herself, and Drew, and the question which waited to be answered.

Briar ducked it with, 'It depends on the circumstances, I suppose.'

Let Drew make what he liked of that. It told him nothing, betrayed nothing. And it took away from him the opportunity to argue.

Ella broke in, 'I don't intend to give up work altogether—it would be a crime to waste all those years of studying for my degree. When the kids get to high school stage, I'll take a refresher course and go back to my research work then. By that time they won't need me to always be there, and I can go back to being me again, as well as being just a mum.' She laughed.

The waiter arrived with the sweet trolley, the talk turned to other topics, and they finished their meal and took their drinks with them to lean against the boat rail and watch the reflection of the lights in the water of the bay.

Briar attached herself to Ella, and the two men followed them across the deck, but when they reached the rail the men parted, Grant going to his wife's side, and Drew coming to lean beside Briar, so close that the sleeve of his dinner-jacket brushed against her bare arm, and sent tingles shooting along it that spilled some of her liqueur into the water below.

'Clumsy of me,' she excused her shaking hand, and sipped at the rest of her drink to hide her confusion. The spirit slid a warm trickle through her, relaxing her rigid muscles.

Grant joked, 'There'll be a few tipsy fish in the harbour tonight!'

The laughter died away, and Drew murmured lazily, 'This is *senang*.' He half turned towards Briar, leaning one elbow against the boat rail, and raised his glass to her with his other hand. 'To...' He paused, his eyes searching her face, before he added slowly, 'To whatever makes you happy.'

Briar was at a loss how to reply. Would she ever know what it was to feel happy again? What she had once believed to be happiness had collapsed round her, as insubstantial as a broken bubble. The future promised her nothing but emptiness.

Make the most of today, her heart urged, and impulsively she grasped at what was left of it, because today was all she had, and to enjoy it would not matter, because tomorrow she would be on a plane back to England—a last-minute cancellation by another hotel guest, which the reception desk had immediately taken up on her behalf.

Recklessly she raised her glass, and with a brittle smile she looked up into Drew's face and repeated his toast, 'To whatever makes you happy.'

His eyes fired, her courage wavered, and hurriedly she digressed, 'What does *senang* mean?'

'Ease. Peace. Bliss. Choose the one that suits you.'

Briar had experienced what she'd once believed to be bliss, and discovered to her cost that it did not last. Ease was for the old. But she could drink to the last, and hope that one day she would find peace.

They danced, and on the cramped space of the cruise boat's deck it was little more than swaying to and fro in each other's arms. She danced with Grant, then she danced with Drew, and he guided her towards the rail, to sway above the water, agleam with reflected light from the deck.

Briar danced woodenly. She held herself stiffly erect, away from him, fearing, and feeling, a return of those electric vibrations which had passed between them during the long hours of the night, when they had kept watch together over the sick child, stronger now because they were closer, held together by Drew's arms.

'What are you afraid of, Briar?'

The question jerked her back to the realisation that Drew too was feeling the vibrations, and his quick perception sensed her fear of them, and responded to it.

The answer she dared not give was that she was afraid of both him and of herself, and even more fearful of the volatile current which flowed between them, which, once it was acknowledged, would explode with a force she might not be able to control.

'Afraid? What is there to be afraid of here?' Briar laughed, a high, unnatural sound. 'We're back in civilisation now. There aren't any bandits here.'

There was one who threatened to take more than she was prepared to give, the danger the more potent because it remained as yet unspoken. Desperately she called on the memory of Philip to help strengthen her resolve.

'I'm tired, I guess,' she borrowed Ella's Americanism.

'We'll be docking soon. There'll be a car waiting, to take us back to the hotel.'

His probing glance said he did not believe her, but to Briar's relief he did not attempt to pursue the matter, and she remained silent as her beleaguered mind confronted yet another problem.

Once they were back at the hotel, she and Drew would be alone together in the executive suite. Would he pursue his question then? And if he did, would she be strong enough to resist the answer? She walked down the steep gangplank beside him, holding on to the rail, which she did not need to steady herself, but used it just the same as an excuse to remain apart from Drew, the while she envied Ella, who walked confidently ahead of her, closed in the shelter of her husband's arm.

They were a perfectly matched pair, the kind who still held hands on their diamond wedding anniversary. But how many couples were so lucky in the lottery of love? Not herself, that was for sure. Her ticket had drawn no prize. It was better to face the future cold than to risk burning her fingers at the same fire twice.

She must cling on to that with both hands, if she was to survive the night ahead. At the last minute, Ella saved her from the necessity. To Briar's surprise, instead of hailing another taxi, Grant helped his wife inside the one Drew had booked. As she settled herself beside Briar, Ella exclaimed, 'Gee, it's good of Drew to offer us an overnight stop. It would be a shame to spoil such a lovely evening by having that long trek back to base.'

Briar could have hugged her. Cheerfully she sorted out a spare nightdress, and shared a final drink, and when she dropped into bed she should have felt reprieved; but instead she felt deprived, and hoped despairingly that when she returned to England her muddled thoughts would sort themselves into some kind of order.

An order she could control. She tried in vain to control her racing pulse when Drew took her to the airport the next morning. She did her utmost to avoid a private parting, hoped he would go with Grant and Ella to the base, but he was adamant.

'I'll drive you to the airport myself.'

At least in the car, he was obliged to keep his attention on the road. But once in that international no man's land of greetings and partings, where public displays of affection were the norm, and not to be frowned on as elsewhere in the city, Drew turned her to face him, and, lowering his dark head above her, sought her lips with his own.

His kiss was everything that her heart had always longed for and never known, and everything which her reason most dreaded. Why did it have to be so searching, delving deep into the very fibres of her being? Why did it have to be so gentle? Why did Drew have to be so unlike Philip in every way? The difference made her want to rejoice, and just as urgently made her want to weep, and all she could manage, in a stifled-sounding voice, was a pleading, 'Drew, don't! Please, don't . . .'

'Why not?' He lifted his head and stared down at her with a perplexed frown. 'What is it that you're afraid of, Briar? There's something between us—you can't deny it. You must have felt it, the same as me. But each time I hold you, you pull away, as if you're afraid. What is it? Tell me, and we can work it out together.'

This was something which she would have to work out alone. But his finger was under her chin, tipping her face up to his, demanding an answer, and she began haltingly, 'Drew, I——'

'Why, if it isn't Mrs Adamson!' A woman's voice, brash, cheerful, and unmistakably Cockney, broke them apart as its owner bustled up, her homely face beaming a welcome.

Drew muttered under his breath, but his face was a bland courtesy as he stood aside to allow the newcomer to greet Briar.

'I haven't seen you for ages,' the woman gushed. 'How's your husband these days? They told me at the clinic you had a little girl.'

A gruff voice called out from the crowd, 'Mavis!' and she grimaced. 'That's hubby—he won't let me out of his sight for five minutes! He's walking nicely now, though, thanks to those exercises you gave him when he smashed his knee. He's been able to go back to his old job at the docks.'

'Mavis!'

'Duty calls,' the newcomer grinned. 'Take care, dearie. Bye!'

'You've got a *husband*? And a *baby*?'

Drew lobbed the accusations at her like hand-grenades through a pool of speaking silence. Briar thought, When they explode, I'll die. She struggled to speak. 'Drew——'

'Don't bother to explain.' Roughly he cut her short. 'A husband and a baby explain themselves. What makes a woman like you tick?' he exploded. 'You're not even a weekend wife. I suppose you condescend to go home for the occasional vacation? Does your baby recognise you when you get there?'

His eyes fixed, gimlet-like, on the ring finger of her left hand, which she raised to cover her trembling lips.

'No wonder you don't wear a wedding-ring! I suppose it makes it easier for you to play the field when you're away from home.'

'You're wrong—quite wrong.'

'Wrong in believing in you,' he grated. 'I should have guessed, when I watched you feeding that baby in the *pondok*. It all came so naturally to you. And no wonder, when you've got a baby of your own! Did you feel fulfilled, like the women's magazines say you should?' he sneered. 'Did it feel good to tend another woman's child, while you left your own behind to take pot luck?'

'Flight 701, to London Heathrow. Will passengers please proceed to the departure lounge?'

The tinny announcement repeated itself in other languages, and Drew spun on his heel. 'See yourself off!' he snarled, and strode away without a backward glance. Without bothering to say goodbye.

Briar watched numbly as the crowd swallowed him up. She wanted to run after him, but her feet fixed her to the floor. She wanted to call after him, but her closed throat would not allow the words to come through. Another, more urgent announcement penetrated her frozen mind.

'Flight 701 to London Heathrow. Will the remaining passenger please proceed *immediately* to the departure lounge.'

That meant herself. If she delayed, she would miss the flight. As if in a dream, Briar picked up her cabin bag and forced her feet in the required direction. Contrarily, now the time had come, she did not want to leave. Not like this. Not with Drew despising her, thinking... Her eyes blurred, and the air hostess pressed the boarding-card into her hand with a sympathetic smile.

She was accustomed to seeing tears of parting. They usually dried quickly enough once the plane took off. The sad-eyed girl with the gentle face and the soft brown curls would feel quite differently by the time they landed at the other end.

Back in Warwick, Briar's eyes were dry, but she felt even worse, if possible, than she had done before. Dutifully she reported on her mission to Tony, and laid out her plans to return to the clinic and her old job, with such a marked lack of enthusiasm that it drew the comment from her brother,

'Why don't you take it easy for a while? Stay and have a holiday, if it's only for a few days. You're still jet lagged.'

'I shall get over it.' Would she ever? 'The quicker I get back into routine, the better. Although, of course, I don't want to leave you short-staffed.'

Belatedly Briar remembered her brother's need, as well as her own, although she suspected that it was one Tony had invented, in order to help her. He confirmed her suspicion with a carefree, 'Don't worry about the business here—it's booming. You

were too tired to talk about it yesterday, so I saved
the best news until now.'

His look said he was bursting to tell, and with
an effort Briar pulled her lips into a smile and invited him, with forced eagerness, 'Tell me.'

'The business has taken off since you've been
away,' Tony enlarged. 'It seems the Steel
Engineering Company were impressed by the
prompt way we bailed Drew out. They've put a lot
more work our way, through their suppliers, and
the whole thing has snowballed to such an extent
that I've given Graham a quick promotion as my
deputy—he was the foreman, remember? He knows
the business inside out, and we're filling the other
vacancies from the bottom. I'm taking on two new
telephone operators. Both of them are partially
sighted. They're smashing workers.'

'Telephone operators? What about Mary?'

'She's redundant,' Tony answered, pan-faced.

'Redundant? Oh, Tony, you can't! Not Mary.
She's been with you for absolutely ages. And she
can't see at all. She may not get another job easily.'

'She's already got one, and thank heaven she's
seen the light at last.' Tony's face relaxed in a broad
grin. 'I can't count the number of times I've asked
her to marry me, and she's always refused, because
of her sight. Now, thank goodness, she's given in
and said yes, and I'm the happiest man alive. So
stop looking as if you'd like to slay me on her
behalf, and come out to dinner with us this evening
to celebrate.'

Briar felt like the proverbial skeleton at the feast,
and, although she remained determinedly cheerful,
Mary's quick perception, heightened by her in-

ability to see, latched on to Briar's underlying depression.

'Are you sure it's only jet lag, Briar?' she questioned gently.

Tony, quick to reassure his bride-to-be, comforted, 'It lasts longer with some people than it does with others. Briar will be fine in a day or two. Have a glass of wine,' he urged his sister. 'It'll buck you up.' He picked up the bottle and read the label out loud, a habit he had acquired in order to keep Mary in the picture. 'Tiger milk. It sounds fierce, but it's a very nice light wine, really. Why, whatever's the matter, Briar?'

'Tiger milk...' Briar choked, and could go no further. In a flash she was back in the jungle, sitting on a longhouse veranda, and listening to a soft Malay voice telling her,

'Such a man is suckled on tiger's milk, to make him stronger than other men.'

Now she was here, in Warwick, and Drew was in Singapore, and the width of the world lay between them, the world of his contempt for the woman he thought her to be, which could not be bridged by an aeroplane.

'Briar, you're crying!' Mary's sharp ear caught her stifled sob. 'Don't bottle it up,' she begged. 'Tell Tony and me. Maybe we can help.'

Drew had urged, 'Tell me, Briar. We can work it out together.'

She had not wanted to work it out, then, because she had been afraid. Now she did, and it never would. Tears rolled unchecked down her cheeks, and the words tumbled disjointedly to mingle with them.

'I love him, Mary—more than I've ever loved anybody before. More than I ever thought I would again. I tried so hard not to, but I can't help myself.'

'Do you mean you love Drew?'

'Yes, oh, yes! I love him, and he despises me. And I don't know what to do.'

'Say you'll marry me, and we can sort out all the rest afterwards,' Drew's voice said from the space directly behind Briar's chair.

Mary said, 'Let's dance, Tony.'

'You haven't finished your sweet yet.'

'I can come back to it later. It's time to dance.'

Mary's hand was on her fiancé's arm, pulling him remorselessly to his feet, and, after one look at his sister's stricken face, Tony complied with a rueful, 'Mary always did see further than me,' and allowed himself to be drawn on to the dance-floor.

'I don't like artificial palms as a rule, but now and then they have their uses,' Drew conceded.

He lifted Briar unceremoniously from her chair and into the shelter of the plastic greenery, with an insincere, 'Sorry to barge in on your private party.'

He did not look in the least sorry, and the cool way in which he had split up their evening roused Briar out of her state of numb shock, to retaliate, 'You've come too late. We'd almost finished eating. It's Tony's treat anyway, not mine. He and Mary have just got engaged.'

'In that case, it looks as if I'll have to treat myself.'

He enjoyed his treat hugely. He plundered her mouth with the hunger of a starving man seeking food. His kiss fused their lips and searched out every throbbing pulse, storming the ramparts of her defences that were no protection as her heart laid down its arms. When he finally raised his head, Briar was pink and gasping.

'That was my starter,' said Drew, and, commandeering Tony's vacant chair, he pulled Briar down on to his knee. 'Now we can talk.'

'What is there to talk about?' she hedged. There was nothing, and everything, and where could they begin?

'You said you loved me—I heard you say it. Twice. So did Tony and Mary. I've got witnesses.'

Briar's cheeks went several shades pinker. 'You despise me.'

'I heard you say that too. And it's not true. But we can talk about that later. You haven't answered my question yet.'

'What question?' She knew, but could not believe it, and she wanted to hear it for a second time too.

'I asked you to marry me. Oh, Briar, I love you so much,' he groaned, and his arms closed round her, crushing her to him. 'That's why I had to keep Lan with us on your last day in the jungle, when all I wanted was to be alone with you. And Grant and Ella, on your last night in Singapore. I love you so much, I daren't trust myself to be alone with you.'

His lips explored the delicate outlines of her face, covering her eyes, her temples, and returning to her mouth as if to their natural home. 'There won't ever be anyone else for me. I loved you the very first moment I set eyes on you.'

'When I came to see you at the Paddocks,' Briar remembered.

'Before then. I drew up beside you in the traffic jam in Warwick. It had to be destiny. There you were, sitting just a few feet away from me, waiting for the traffic-lights to change. And I knew, then, that you were the girl I'd waited for all my life.'

The grey Jaguar. Memory returned to Briar as Drew went on, 'I trailed you until you turned into Tony's yard, and the moment I got home I telephoned with the excuse that I needed help, and simply prayed you would be the one to come. I couldn't believe my luck when you did. Nor when you told me you hadn't got any commitments.'

Briar murmured low, 'I did have commitments. But not any more.'

'I know—I heard about that later. After we parted at the airport.' Drew's face paled at the memory of that parting.

'How did you find out?'

'Do you remember the big, chatty woman who rushed up and buttonholed you?' Briar nodded. Would she ever forget her? 'When her husband called out to her, he was trying to stop her from talking to you. He'd heard about your divorce, and about poor little Lucy, from the clinic.'

His arms folded her closer, cradling her against the pain of that time. 'He didn't tell his wife about it before they came away on holiday, for fear the news might depress her. It seems they both got very fond of you, during their visits to the clinic. Oh, my darling, how did you bear it?' Drew cupped her face in his hands and turned it up to meet his, a pale flower between his long, tanned fingers.

'If only you'd let me comfort you! I longed to hold you in my arms, and kiss away the pain in your eyes. I didn't know what had caused it, and you wouldn't tell me, and all the time it was Philip, and little Lucy.'

'Lucy, not Philip. That pain faded a long time ago.'

The tears flowed again, but this time they were warm tears, healing tears, and she did not mind Drew seeing them. He reached into his pocket and pulled out a handkerchief, and wiped them gently away.

'My handkerchief!' Briar exclaimed. 'So the laundry returned it, after all?' Her blurred eyes focused on the embroidered rose.

'The laundry never had it in the first place,' Drew confessed. 'I stole it, to take with me into the jungle. I couldn't bear to leave you. I had to have something of yours, to take with me.'

'I kept the sarong you lent me.'

'I bought it for you, to give to you when I got back to Singapore. You just had your present a bit earlier, that's all.'

Briar said slowly, 'When I followed you, I really did think Ranjit would come back for me the same day.' She had to make that clear between them.

'I knew that all along. I believed you.'

'You shouted at me.'

'Will you ever forgive me?' His lips sought, and received, forgiveness, as he confessed, 'I shouted at you, because I was so afraid for you. You were so vulnerable. I couldn't bear the thought that harm might come to you. You'd got no defence against things like malaria, and caterpillars...'

A bubble of laughter broke inside Briar. 'And tigers?' she added mischievously.

'There weren't any tigers on the island.'

'There was one. They called him Balang.'

Their laughter mingled, then Briar dried her face with the rose-embroidered handkerchief, and when she went to tuck it into her pocket, its work done, Drew claimed it for his own.

'I want to keep it in my wallet, to carry with me whenever I have to be away from you, even for a moment.'

'I've got the little piece of parchment to carry with me—the one you gave me with the Chinese writing on it. You told me it was a kind of promise.' Suddenly she felt shy of asking, and, loving her shyness, Drew relented, and interpreted for her.

'Translated loosely, it says, "I love you forever". That was the promise bit. But I didn't know how you'd take it. I was afraid it might scare you off if I hurried you too much. So I had it put in writing so you could carry my promise with you, even though you didn't know what it meant. Do you want it spelt out word for word? It sounds much more formal in Chinese.'

Briar shook her head contentedly. 'No. "I love you forever" is enough.'

A long, preoccupied silence passed, then Drew said, 'By the way, the baby from the longhouse was recovering nicely when I left Singapore. Oh, and Tim sends his love. Elizabeth and Robert rang me before I left. Robert's enjoying his holiday so much, he's wondering why he hasn't had one before.'

'That's the best possible news. Running off with Tim worked.'

'I was desperate to do anything that would bring Robert to his senses and save their marriage. When you came on the scene it seemed the perfect answer to begin to plan my own,' he smiled.

Briar showed him her precious picture of Lucy. Drew studied it gravely for a while, then with gentle fingers he closed the clasp of the locket, closing a chapter of her life, and opening up another with the tender promise,

'I'll give you another Lucy.'

'We won't call her Lucy. I'm not superstitious, but——'

'We'll call her Rose. It goes nicely with Briar.'

'I'd like a family—like Ella. Not just one.'

'We'll have as many as you want, and not one of them will ever compare with you.' Suddenly Drew sobered. 'Something Ella said set me thinking.' At Briar's look of enquiry, he added slowly, 'She said she wanted to be herself, not just a mum.' Earnestly he gazed into her face. 'I wouldn't want to stop you from being yourself when you marry me. I wouldn't make things difficult for you if you wanted to carry on working. There's plenty of money for us to employ a nursemaid to look after our children. They would still have a settled, secure home. Secure in our love.'

With his words muffled by kisses, Drew begged, 'I'd rather have you as a weekend wife than not have you at all.'

Briar's arms rose to twine themselves round his neck, as they had longed to do before, but had been prevented by her fear. Pressing his face close to her own, she stopped his stumbling words with her lips.

'A family of children will keep me fully occupied at home,' she declared. 'I'd want to look after them myself, especially while they were little. Afterwards, when they go to college, I might do the same as Ella then, and take a refresher course and go back to part-time work. But there's plenty of time between then and now. All the time in the world,' she said contentedly.

His eyes fired. 'Does that mean you'll marry me?'

'I means I'll marry you.'

'This is *senang*,' Drew breathed, and claimed her lips as they parted to agree.

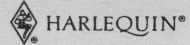 HARLEQUIN®

THE TAGGARTS OF TEXAS!

Harlequin's Ruth Jean Dale brings you
THE TAGGARTS OF TEXAS!

Those Taggart men—strong, sexy and hard to resist...

You've met Jesse James Taggart in FIREWORKS!
Harlequin Romance #3205 (July 1992)

Now meet Trey Smith—he's THE RED-BLOODED YANKEE!
Harlequin Temptation #413 (October 1992)

Then there's Daniel Boone Taggart in SHOWDOWN!
Harlequin Romance #3242 (January 1993)

And finally the Taggarts who started it all—in LEGEND!
Harlequin Historical #168 (April 1993)

Read all the Taggart romances!
Meet all the Taggart men!

Available wherever Harlequin books are sold.

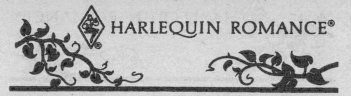

HARLEQUIN ROMANCE®

Valerie Bloomfield comes home to Orchard Valley, Oregon, for the saddest of reasons. Her father has suffered a serious heart attack, and now his three daughters are gathering at his side, praying he'll survive.

Orchard Valley

This visit home will change Valerie's life—especially when she meets Colby Winston, her father's handsome and strong-willed doctor!

"The Orchard Valley trilogy features three delightful, spirited sisters and a trio of equally fascinating men. The stories are rich with the romance, warmth of heart and humor readers expect, and invariably receive, from Debbie Macomber."

—Linda Lael Miller

Don't miss the Orchard Valley trilogy by Debbie Macomber:

VALERIE Harlequin Romance #3232 (November 1992)
STEPHANIE Harlequin Romance #3239 (December 1992)
NORAH Harlequin Romance #3244 (January 1993)

Look for the special cover flash on each book!

Available wherever Harlequin books are sold   ORC-G

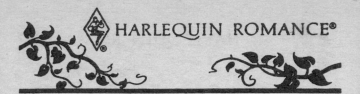